CW00591532

DARK KNIGHTS OF COMPTON BERRY

Wendy Ruocco

To Chris + Rachel love from Wendy x

Published by:
Wendy Ruocco
44 Davies Avenue, Whiterock, Paignton, Devon, TQ4 7AP

British Library Cataloguing-in-Publication Data.
A catalogue record for this book is available
from the British Library.

This is a work of fiction. Names, characters, places and incidents are
the product of the author's imagination and any resemblance to actual
persons, living or dead, events or locales, is purely coincidental.

Dedication:
For all the medieval heroes who
strode through my dreams

ISBN 978-0-9554942-0-8
Printed in Great Britain by
Arthur H. Stockwell Ltd.
Torrs Park   Ilfracombe
Devon

Dark Knights of Compton Berry

The flowers of the field were shining brightly in the summer sunshine as Faye picked her way along the leafy footpath. At the bottom of the lane, where the foliage thinned, the light was blinding, and Faye had to shield her eyes from the glare of the buttercup-filled meadow.

Catching her breath at the wonder of the sight, she thought again of Ciabhan, and how she wished he'd chosen to accompany her this afternoon, but more pressing manor business had needed his attention. . . .

She remembered him looking over her shoulder at the manuscript spread before her on the escritoire. She recalled also, with a smile, his lips dangerously close to her ear as he'd teased, "Am I mentioned at all, my sweet?"

Disappointed by his refusal to join her, she had gently pushed his head away, and with mock scolding had replied, "Do you think you should be, sir?"

Before she could react he had kissed her ear. Backing away quickly, just before her hand struck air, he had laughingly said, "I hope a mere kiss will not be denied when we are wed, madam, or will you become a harridan who beats and scolds her husband?"

Exasperated, she twisted to speak but he had already left, and through the open door his chuckles could be heard from the stairwell.

Invitingly the sun shone through her window, seeming to beckon her outside; maybe her writing could wait after all on such a splendid day . . .

A few days only had passed since she and Ciabhan walked together through these very meadows. Knee-deep in buttercups, they had delighted in each other's company, believing they alone existed in this magical yellow wonderland.

Later, as the day had mellowed and violet shadows lengthened, they had strolled back through dappled lanes, grass and red earth staining their summer tunics, and necks and noses pink from the sun. Like two mischievous peasant children they had giggled at the curious stares of the villagers, Faye hotly clutching a drooping bunch of golden cups. . . .

Taking care not to slip in the muddy puddles bordering the shallow but fast-flowing stream, Faye crossed cautiously on the stepping stones that rose just high enough to keep her feet dry. On reaching the other side she removed her sandals, and let the refreshing water wash over her toes. Savouring the peace of the clearing, she watched as her feet turned paler and paler. Not bothering to dry her feet, she rose and, minding the stinging nettles that crowded the gap in the hedge, stepped out of the cool into the sea of gold.

Faye's idea of paradise existed in a world of nature's most beautiful greens and yellows, the colours of spring and rebirth, the colours of her happy childhood. Growing to womanhood in the rural idyll of Devon, life was suffused by these colours. Through boughs heavy with soft blossoms or glimpsed over hedgerows, hues of every green blended with rose-red soil. Called Faye for the faery spirits she resembled as a small girl, her childhood dreams had been inspired by her beloved countryside. In that meadow she stood alone and thought back on the events of the recent years. . . .

It seemed those dreams had now come true, for in reality a champion now strode beside her – Ciabhan – not a figment of her imagination, but a flesh-and-blood man, who had turned her world and his upside down; a man for whom she had risked her reputation; and a man whose life had been nearly lost for love of her. It would not be long before she would marry Sir Ciabhan of Compton Berry, the man she adored.

A year ago he had left Faye in the keeping of his great friend and ally, Brother Ivan. After a long absence, Ciabhan had returned, having successfully petitioned the Holy See of Rome for an annulment of Faye's first marriage to Leon. At last free to marry, she looked forward to becoming Ciabhan's wife – the wife of a fallen Knight Templar.

The idea of documenting the story of their love had grown from her months of loneliness spent at Compton Berry. She wished to show that ultimately fate alone dictated the paths of desire. Once the path was set upon, nothing would stop that which was predestined.

Ciabhan, meanwhile, in his private chamber couldn't have been further away in mind. Idly he toyed with the short-handled dagger that lay on a soft chamois in front of him, trying to focus on more pressing concerns.

Since his return from Rome he had noticed a strain in the relationship between the two people that mattered most to him – his great friend and comrade-in-arms, Ivan; and Faye, Ciabhan's bride-to-be, the woman for whom he would willingly lay down his life. Surely there could be no problem between his two greatest friends. Possibly it was his imagination that the castle seemed to be in a state of tension, waiting as when a storm threatens, bubbling and brewing on the horizon, but never quite breaks. On his return, Ivan had welcomed him back with great warmth and enthusiasm, and Faye had fallen into his arms weeping, her relief evident.

Ciabhan sighed wearily and pushed his chair away from the table. Stretching his legs he winced as the effort pulled at his thigh wound. Slumping lower into the carved chair, he placed his fingertips together, lowered his head to them and closed his eyes allowing his thoughts free rein.

The late afternoon sun touched everything with a coppery glow as it slanted onto the trappings of domesticity. Ciabhan's silver goblet, engraved with scenes of Jerusalem, a present from Ivan, held the rays in a groove, while a trickle of wine coursed its way downwards creating a little river of shimmering blood.

As the room flooded with light, the polished hilt of Ciabhan's dagger flashed and religious objects dotted around the room became gilded, giving the chamber the feel of a divine sanctuary. In its centre the almost godlike figure of Ciabhan rested. Tanned from weeks in the open air, his skin glowed with health, and spirituality seemed to surround him, which enhanced his obvious masculinity.

His looks were Norman, as was his birth. Aquiline features of a long straight nose and hard mouth were softened by expressive brown eyes. Small crinkles at their sides proved that a smile, if rare, was not totally unknown to this knight. Good skin was mostly hidden by a trim moustache and beard, greying very slightly as was his long brown hair.

Burnishing all it touched, the rays of the sun filtered through his chestnut hair with its little flecks of grey and highlighted the golden nape of his neck, creating what appeared to be a halo. Oblivious of the surreal scene, Ciabhan sighed and stretched languorously, reaching for the goblet at his left hand.

He would speak with his friend tomorrow, after Mass in the chapel. Ciabhan and Ivan enjoyed a unique friendship, and always found time to talk, whether in peace or wartime, or fatigued after battle, in hope and in despair, in anger and unity. Ciabhan was the consummate Knight Templar, hero of Christianity, back from the Holy Land covered in glory; and Brother Ivan was the would-be Templar, scholar and theologian, educated and intellectual but thwarted in his dreams of knighthood.

Draining the cup of wine, Ciabhan rose and crossed to the window. Inhaling the sweet air he looked out over dense green treetops and beyond to the valley where the lower track wound its way past the woodsmen's cottages, skirted the larch wood and ended its path in the muddy stream. Yes, he would definitely talk with Ivan as soon as was possible. For now, though, why spoil such a lovely evening? Above his head newly arrived swifts circled and swooped screeching into the roof recesses where they had nested for years. Always fascinated by these summer visitors, he observed their acrobatics, familiar with their dipping and diving from the many hours spent close to them on battlements in lonely castles. He watched captivated as they soared high into the dry air, only to plunge earthwards, their shrill calls hanging in the stillness. As Ciabhan gazed upon the aerial antics, the door to the chamber swung inwards, creaking on its heavy hinges. From the darkening void beyond its opening, an even darker form stepped. Ciabhan turned slowly, reluctant to leave the display outside his window.

Coming towards him, both hands outstretched in greeting, was his friend and companion Brother Ivan, already halfway across the room. Fine particles of dust having lain undisturbed, rose and swirled around him as his cloak brushed surfaces. Shimmering like prisms, they danced through the shafts of sunlight, scattering before Ivan as he advanced smiling towards Ciabhan.

The foreign-looking man was Ciabhan's friend and fellow knight, Ivan. The two men differed greatly in looks. The visitor's slight and wiry frame seemed on first sight to be that of a cleric, but the black he favoured hid the honed physique of a fighting man, and the most striking thing about him was his hair. Long, straight and black as a raven's wing, it framed his dusky clean-shaven features in a cascade of glossy ink. Flashing a brilliant smile Ivan said warmly, "My lord," and stooped to kiss the back of Ciabhan's hand.

As he did so he noticed the circle of pale skin where

once the great emerald had flashed – the same emerald as that whose perfection had gleamed on Faye's finger for so many months. Now the far-from-perfect gem lay shattered in Faye's chamber, its beauty cracked and flawed, a silent reminder of guilt.

Ciabhan welcomed his friend with enthusiasm: "My dear Ivan! Come, take some wine with me. I am a little melancholy; you are just the tonic! It's too long since we shared an hour or two!"

Ciabhan poured some wine and offered it. Ivan took the cup, swirling the ruby liquid before lifting it to his lips. They stood opposite each other in the window alcove, an odd silence dividing them. Ivan avoided his friend's gaze, unwilling to meet those trusting brown eyes. He looked skywards and prayed for strength, but as the warm light faded so did his hopes of confessing his torment.

Ciabhan's handsome features darkened with irritation. He hadn't fought the heathen and survived battles in far-flung places by being a fool, and God help any who thought him one! With an edge of impatience he spoke to the gloomy Ivan: "In God's name what ails you, Brother. You seem to have the weight of the world on your shoulders!" Ciabhan was the taller and broader of the two. He leant towards the younger man. Concerned for his friend's discomfort, he was still a master of diplomacy. His eyes glittered intensely and his jaw set as he persisted: "Ivan, as much as I love you, my patience is wearing a little thin!" The hint of a smile broke the hard line of his mouth.

Ivan remained silently brooding. Olive-skinned, he had a slight look of the East about him. High cheekbones set off a wide and sensual mouth, while beneath the curtain of black hair, alert and intelligent eyes flashed like the rarest black diamonds. Known as the Raven he was as usual clothed from head to foot in black.

Nature had blessed both men with exceptional good looks. Where Ivan exuded an air of the exotic, Ciabhan epitomised the perfect knight. Nearly six foot tall, he possessed the strong body of a warrior, and the character to match. Their bond of friendship had proved unshakeable; side by side, on and off the battlefield, as brothers in arms they had supported one another, so the tension between them now was all the more noticeable.

Ivan, aware of his friend's attempts at tolerance, abandoned any ideas of confession and, with an effort unnoticed by Ciabhan, answered, "It is true I have been a little preoccupied of late, but I came to suggest we go hawking tomorrow. The weather looks set fair. How feel you, My Lord? A pleasure overdue for the two of us?"

Ciabhan straightened, swept a coil of damp hair from his forehead and threw his arm around Ivan's shoulder. "Why not, my friend. A pleasure overdue indeed! Maybe Faye would care to join us."

High above the bustle of the dining hall, smoke from the fire swirled around the rafters before finding its way through gaps in the roof and escaping into the balmy evening. Below this haze the hall was alive with noise and confusion. Voices rose and fell as children competed with the scavenging hounds to be heard. Orders were given and objections muttered as tempers flared and died. From this seeming chaos would come the evening meal, when each member of the household, in degrees of importance, would take their place at benches laden with plenty. Once satiated, they would make their way to bed, or sleep where they fell, leaving master and guests to talk and drink into the night, the mistress and ladies having long taken their leave of any rowdiness.

Embracing the tendrils of smoke snaking from the upper reaches of the hall, delicious cooking smells joined the silent exodus and drifted down through the valley, permeating the air with the promise of well-fed stomachs, peace and prosperity.

Reaching the senses of Faye, this reminder of time jolted her from her dreaming. Was it really this hour? She must have been asleep, for the last thing she remembered was the twittering and furtive rustlings of wildlife in the

9

undergrowth. Now, adjusting her eyes to the cloak of ultramarine that night had draped about her, she slowly became aware of how quickly two (or was it three?) hours had slipped away from her.

A slight breeze shook the leaves above her head, bringing a chill to her skin. Shivering, she pulled her wrap around bare shoulders and, gathering the limp buttercups, she eased herself to her feet. Finally alert, she retraced her steps back up the steep and rutted path to where welcoming light emanated from the castle.

The last few steps brought her to the huge and ancient oak; for years lovers had carved their lovers' names in its trunk. She smiled knowing that her and Ciabhan's were also there. Locked within a heart the names Faye and Ciabhan would live on for as long as the tree itself; maybe for hundreds of years people would pass by and wonder.

Passing under the arched gate, Faye shuddered. Always cool beneath the dank shadow, its shade felt particularly damp after this lovely day. She acknowledged the guard's greeting with a wave and hurried on, past the stables clustered along the walls, and past the piles of steaming dung.

Torches flared in their sconces and light from the bright flames danced on the activities of the outer bailey as Faye looked up to Ciabhan's chamber. Noticing a light in his window, she changed her mind and headed towards the covered stairway that would take her through the painted chapel and along the narrow passageway to Ciabhan's room – his sanctuary, he called it. A few moments alone with her betrothed before the dining-hall clatter would be precious indeed!

She was anticipating this meeting as she entered the chapel. Usually Brother Ivan would be there, but tonight she was surprised to find it empty. Normally at this hour, Brother Ivan would be at prayer or busying himself within the tranquillity of the manor's chapel, and candles would have been burning in the wall brackets. Just one lonely candle cast its flame upon the small marble altar. Briefly

Faye considered checking the lower chamber where Ivan slept, but as no light filtered upwards she decided against further investigation and continued along the narrow passageway, a little puzzled.

Just before the steps leading to Ciabhan's private chamber a small recess was used by the guards who took turns at his personal watch. Faye acknowledged the guard with a warm smile and a "Good evening." Keeping her eyes on the uneven flagstones in the half-light, she began to mount the steps. As she climbed she was suddenly aware of a form obscuring the little light above her. Leaning for support into the wall, a dark shape was descending the stairs, unaware of her presence. For seconds she thought it an apparition and gasped, her hand flying to her mouth to stifle a scream. Shaken, she managed a weak "Who goes there?" but almost immediately she knew who approached. "Ivan! By all the saints, you scared me half to death!"

Against the dreary walls his face had a haunted look and the hollows beneath his eyes appeared exceptionally dark – maybe just a trick of the light.

With her heart still pounding in her throat and ears, she said, "I thought you a ghost!"

Ivan only stared impassively back at her, his expression sad.

Smiling, she reached to touch his cheek, a gesture of reassurance, before asking gently, "And how does My Lord Ivan. All is well, I trust?" A moment's panic swept through her, knowing he had just come from Ciabhan. Urgently, now she said, "Tell me, Brother: there is no problem, I hope?"

Ivan's body relaxed and, as if suddenly aware of her presence, he looked into her hazel eyes, removed her hand from his cheek and kissed her fingers, making no attempt to release them.

Echoing around the stairwell, the drip of water sounded strangely loud as it oozed from the moisture-laden ferns clinging to the walls.

They stood where they had met, her fingers in his hand,

11

the silence broken only by their breathing. The sudden proximity of their bodies in such an enclosed space made both slightly uncomfortable.

Letting go of her hand, Ivan answered finally, "He is well, in excellent health and humour. Your presence, Faye, can only better that."

She smiled, but looked with concern at him. "And you, Ivan? You are a little pale."

Avoiding her eyes, he lied: "News from Rome – all is not well with my mother."

"I'm sorry to hear that," Faye said.

"And I'm sorry if I frightened you just now. Forgive me?" he said.

"My dear, Ivan, I could never have anything to forgive you for," she said light-heartedly, half expecting a smile to crease his face, but without another word he turned and was gone.

Faye considered the strange encounter for a moment. If it were not for his scent of patchouli that hung heavy in the air, she might have thought their meeting a dream. With a puzzled backward glance, Faye climbed the remaining steps to Ciabhan's chamber, her thoughts already moving ahead.

A turquoise-encrusted mirror hung exotically over an oak bench on the small landing outside Ciabhan's room, and Faye stopped to check her reflection. Shaking her hair free of its clip, she let it tumble over her shoulders, then, adjusting her wrap and smoothing her skirts, she stepped into the room.

Ciabhan's spirits lifted even more as his eyes fell on this latest welcome visitor. It took Faye only moments to cross the room into Ciabhan's arms.

Below, in the darkening chapel, Ivan had already prostrated himself on the floor in front of the altar. At last ready to meet his demons, he was oblivious of the cold creeping up through his body from the ancient stones or the shadows that chased across the walls and painted ceiling. Alone the noble Raven lay, wretched and desolate.

After dinner that evening, when all had retired and the castle slumbered within the deafening silence of the green woods, Faye rose from bed, her slippered feet carrying her as a moth to the light. Like a whisper on the breeze, she crossed the bailey to the chapel.

The long night that Faye was to endure with Ivan gave her hours in which to reflect on the circumstances that had bound the three of them together, once fate had taken a hand, binding what no mortal could break.

Once again she stroked Ivan's shoulder, her touch reassuring him of her presence, as his body jerked free of another demon.

"You are not alone, Ivan. All will be well."

This night would allow plenty of time for reflection. Shivering at the draughts which blew unexpectedly, she huddled deep into her shawl, trying to ignore the furtive tappings that echoed from the shadowy passageway and dark recesses. With difficulty she dismissed the flickering candle when the flame rose and fell, as if someone invisible had passed through it, as another figment of her imagination.

Only once was she really scared: on giving way to welcome sleep, her loose hair was pulled almost playfully by an unseen hand! Instantly alert, she looked slowly around expecting to see Ciabhan! But no, just another draught or demon maybe? She knew she deserved to suffer along with the man prone before her, but these tricks of the mind were hard to bear.

As the night's vigil wore on, Faye drew on the comfort of good memories and the friendship between her, Ciabhan and Ivan, but always not far from the surface was the memory of her betrayal of Ciabhan. The thought of it made her weep in the silent chapel. The guilt bubbled and simmered like a cauldron of poison about to boil over, as if waiting to pollute the perfect harmony they had enjoyed.

Faye accepted her guilt and her shame readily, but for comfort in that dark place she forced her mind back to the beginning.

Faye, gently watching over Ivan, shared the torment afflicting him as she confronted her own demons. She listened as Ivan's breathing came in noisy painful bursts. . . .

Nothing stirred as the Raven flew low through the woods in the valley, over the tall larch and out of their shadow. His spirit free of his broken body and as light as the air, he soared ever upwards into the black void, above all living things on the back of the wind – alone in his greatest fight.

Instinctively the Raven knew that, without this exorcism, he would never survive the night; but he was certain that if his heart should break, welcome death would deliver him from this earthly suffering for ever. Mortal love had been the cause of this pain. Now he fought to be free of it! Time was non-existent as the fight raged within his anguished soul. Higher and higher the glistening black wings carried him over ever diminishing images of the earth. When exhaustion finally descended, his torment ceased as thermals carried him far beyond pain, numbing his failing consciousness.

The last demon took flight from his tortured spirit as Sunrise appeared rosy on the horizon, replacing viridian shadows with hues of softest lime and draping all she touched in a cloth of gold and pink. Radiant Dawn advanced over the countryside, driving night's terrors before her, and promising another glorious day. For seconds she danced along the high ramparts, adorning the cold stones with colour before splintering down through the chapel's tinted glass panes, and coming to rest like droplets of blood on the blue-black hair which lay in damp strands around the face of the man on the cold stone floor. . . .

Through the night Faye kept vigil over Ivan, feeling every painful spasm that wracked his body.

Just before dawn arrived, the candle spluttered and died. Quickly she rose and lit another; Ivan would not wake in darkness. It was the only time she moved from her chair during the long night's vigil, until, as silently as she came, she made her way back to her bed chamber, God willing, to sleep awhile.

Even in her wildest dreams, Faye could never have guessed at the twists and turns fate had had in store for her. She had been happily married for many years to Leon on the day she first met the famous Knight Templar, Sir Ciabhan of Compton Berry.

That meeting would bring their links to Ivan.

Allowing her thoughts to flow freely, she savoured each moment and every word of that fateful day. . . .

The homecoming of her husband, Leon, had brought visitors to her small courtyard. Assembled in a riot of colour and clamour they awaited their grooms and servants to take charge of the mounts and arms so that the hospitalities could begin in earnest. To be graced with the presence of such a knight as Sir Ciabhan was a great honour for Leon and his wife.

Wrapped in her husband's arms, where he'd lifted her onto his saddle, she'd become aware of the trio of riders in the middle of the group. Aloof from their travelling companions they waited patiently to be unarmed while others around them fretted and swore. A very impressive knight sat looking haughtily in their direction astride the most magnificent destrier that Faye had ever seen. Nuzzling closer to her husband, where she had climbed into his arms, Faye asked, "And who is the fellow over there, my love?" pointing to the group. "He looks very fierce."

Leon looked indulgently at his wife. The face he had yearned to gaze on so often while away was now bright with curiosity. Her hazel eyes shone with excitement and little flecks of green danced within their depths. The green always appeared more intense when she wore her favourite colour, and today in Leon's honour she had donned a gown of mossy green velvet. It complemented her honeyed skin and showed to perfection the amber torque around her neck. Opaque droplets and small seed pearls hung from the golden circlet. Caressing the back of her neck he replied, "He, my precious, is the Templar, Sir Ciabhan of Compton Berry."

Faye had shivered at his touch as, giggling, she had replied, "Maybe so, sir, but he is not the most handsome for that man is here in my arms!"

He bent and kissed her forehead. Leon knew that his wife could be headstrong and impudent – a natural exuberance that was sometimes misinterpreted. He tilted her chin and whispered in his heavily accented half English and half French, "Now, now, my sweet, you must be courteous to our guest. He is here at my invitation, and is the bravest man I have ever had the honour of serving under. He is, I grant you, arrogant, but valiant and chivalrous as a Knight Templar should be; and it is a privilege to have him stay here."

Disentangling herself from Leon's arms, she turned to see the Templar better, only to find him almost at her side.

With an exaggerated bow from the saddle and a look of disdain, he removed his gauntlet and extended his hand to her in greeting, addressing her thus: "An honour to meet you, my lady. Pray tell me," he nodded at Leon, "is this the way the lady of the house greets all her guests?"

A ripple of laughter spread through the hushed group of men.

Quite unprepared for the mocking tone of his voice, Faye had taken his outstretched hand and, maintaining eye contact, had elegantly dismounted from her precarious foothold on the stirrup of Leon's mount, still with her hand in Ciabhan's grip!

The difference in the height of seated knight and the ground seriously upset his balance and Faye felt the panic in his fingers, and saw the alarm flit across his face. At full stretch, and at the mercy of this small woman, he realised that with just a little more pressure he would be an undignified heap at her feet.

For a moment Faye held the dignity of the knight in her hand and felt his softening. Smiling, she held his deep-brown eyes with hers. Then, lowering them modestly, she replied humbly, "My Lord, if a kiss is what you desire, then it would be my pleasure. However, you will have to bend a little closer!" She held his hand a moment longer, giving him time to regain his balance. Rising gracefully, Faye made the most of the situation, and she dared to say, "Surely even a Knight Templar is permitted to kiss the hand of his host's wife?"

Although tender from being so long in his grip, she still smiled triumphantly as his lips brushed the skin on the back of her hand.

Sir Ciabhan had been man enough to rise to the challenge and acknowledged, possibly for the first time in his life, defeat at the hands of a mere woman! Undaunted by her teasing, he had the last word. "My Lady, I concede; you win!" Quietly, so only she heard, he whispered, "This time!" To Leon who had been watching the proceedings with wry amusement, he said, "A spirited woman indeed, my friend – a match for any man – however, a Templar monk is a different matter!" Then, almost as an afterthought, he added, "Neither does your description do her beauty justice, my dear Leon."

Faye remembered how the gusty wind had played havoc with her hair on that day: unbound it tangled around their joined hands. Looking back it seemed no accident that he held her in his grip for a fraction longer than was appropriate – time enough for her to notice the stunning emerald gleaming on his finger beneath her windswept hair. Saluting her formally, he had whirled in a cloud of dust back to his bemused companions. For once lost for words, Faye could only look speechless at the ground. . . .

The encounter had been her first with Ciabhan, and during the night's vigil the memory had given comfort, even with her mind in turmoil. She was glad she had started a record of their lives; it was to be her gift to Ciabhan on their wedding day – their story. . . .

The arrival of guests had called for celebration and the

evening meal was a lively one. Alone amongst the company of males she listened to the tales of gallantry and the feats of honour as old battles were recounted. When one of the group was proved to have exaggerated his prowess they bayed with laughter, leaving the wretch to wish he had never opened his mouth.

The evening, as usual, became boisterous. A young member of the company had been dowsed in ale, mocked and kicked about the room while most present roared with laughter.

The Templar had been placed between herself and Leon. To Faye he was polite, picking his words carefully and speaking mostly to Leon.

Also dining was the odious Halbert, a man most loathed but tolerated. He was the son of elderly Sir Ralf of Boscombe Valle; but unlike his father, who was a kind and benevolent man, Halbert was detested, and the only incident that had marred the evening was because of him. Sir Ralf appeared unaware of the contempt most felt for his son. It was to Halbert's father that Leon owed fealty, and, in return for his loyalty, Sir Ralf had eventually allowed Leon to purchase the small manor by the sea in Pagons Ton.

Contemplating a last visit to his birthplace in Normandy Sir Ralf wished Leon to escort him, and he had said, "Be prepared, Leon. Before next summer is over I will wish to see Normandy, but until then, my dear," he'd addressed Faye mischievously, "you have him all to yourself!"

Out of his father's sight, Halbert had sneered to his cronies, "That's assuming the old fool lives that long!"

Faye had particularly enjoyed the melancholy songs of the little Welsh minstrel. He'd accompanied his songs with dramatic gestures and Faye had hummed along with the tunes, ignoring the sniggers of Halbert. It made her angry that such disrespect could be shown for the man and his art. Looking down the table, she hissed her displeasure at Halbert, "Manners obviously are a virtue unknown to you, sir!"

Fixing her with watery blue eyes, Halbert had replied, "The Welsh, in case you hadn't noticed, madam, are all mountain goats. One does not compliment them! French is the only tongue of civilised people, for song and for passion." He grinned lasciviously before skewering a bloody piece of venison into his mouth. Faye turned away revolted as, with his mouth open, he threw back his head and laughed, the juice running down his unshaven chin.

By her side the Templar's eyes narrowed. Not giving credence to Halbert's comment, he stared straight ahead.

As Faye prepared to take her leave from the assembled diners, Leon had whispered softly in her ear, understanding completely his wife's anger with Halbert. "Well done, My Lady. He really isn't worthy of your hate. Come, take my arm; let me escort you."

Addressing the assembled diners, she said, "Welcome, guests. Please excuse my leaving. This day has been long and – here she hesitated, shooting a look at the Templar who lowered his dark eyes – for a mere woman, an extremely exciting one. Please continue to enjoy our hospitality. Tomorrow, for those wishing a diversion, there is plentiful hunting in the woods, or a day of hawking. Now I wish you all a very good night."

Leon breathed a sigh of relief. He had hoped his wife would not react to Halbert's baiting or provoke the Templar further. She had instead smiled demurely when all had risen to bid her goodnight.

For most of the night Faye had lain listening to the revelry in the hall, eventually falling asleep. She never recalled Leon coming to bed but, snoring like a pig and smelling like one, he was there when she awoke with the dawn.

Bending, she kissed him on the forehead. He grunted and rolled dangerously near the edge of the bed! "Good," thought Faye aloud, "that will wake you, my sweet lord."

From the bowl of refreshing rose water on her washstand she cleansed the night away and dressed. Quietly, so as not to waken him at this stage, she slipped along the wooden gallery, past the other two chambers where guests slept, and down the steps that led directly into the garden. Stepping warily over bodies collapsed where they had fallen, she thankfully left behind the overpowering smell of ale, wine and unwashed bodies.

Even now she could almost taste that delicious morning. The sun had risen over the wooded hills, curving away to the north-east in a shimmering orb of silver. Glistening on the still waters of the bay, it cast a line of blinding light along the horizon, between heaven and earth. As if all the saints in heaven had descended at once, the new day birthed in brilliant quicksilver.

Enchanted, Faye had moved through all this beauty as if she were the only person alive on earth.

Just before turning into the orchard, she glanced back at the home she had just left. Built of soft Devon sandstone, it sat just beyond the flat shoreline of this sheltered bay. The same sandstone had been used to build the church and the palace of the bishops, the tower of which rose just above the trees in the orchard, the pennants still in the morning's listless air. Occasionally the fat little Bishop of Exeter visited, bringing his entourage with him, and turning the palace grounds into a bustling hive of industry. Faye had loved the markets that were held there on celebration days, when traders from all over would gather with their wares, selling the unusual and the exotic. She liked to collect trinkets and jewels, spices and unguents for wounds from far-flung places, pretty pieces of material and coloured glass. The little blue and green Venetian-glass bird that sat on her window ledge shining in the morning sun was bought for her by Leon; and the amber necklace she wore yesterday for his return had come from this very market, sold by a strange little man in a straw hat and bright orange robes. He had said in his very poor French, "Love lady, this bon on you neck – come, you try!" Intrigued, Faye had let him place it around her neck, then marvelled at its mysterious depths as he explained the secrets of the little pieces of moss and insects that lay for ever trapped in its honeyed centre. She now had many beads of amber lovingly collected as gifts. Some shone in her ears or on her wrists, or sometimes in her hair. Over the years she had looked often for the funny little man, but she never saw him or his like again. Sometimes she wondered about the cold places to the north where he had said the best amber could be picked off the shore. She imagined it lying golden in the sun, guarding for ever its captured secrets.

Through the orchard she had walked beneath the blossom-laden branches where birds chattered and played. Within the tracery of boughs the blue sky peeped and dappled the dewy grass beneath her feet. With utter joy in her step she crossed to the mews looking forward to a few moments with Bella Donna before the household woke and broke the peace.

The door to the mews was in need of repair and she had mentioned it to the reeve. Still, she had been a little surprised to find it half open and took care when entering, feeling she was not alone. Adjusting her eyes to the gloom she heard only the squawking and flapping of the hawks as they became restless at her intrusion.

At the far end of the shed the Templar turned his gaze to meet Faye's. Focusing, she saw that Bella Donna devoured hungrily a juicy titbit he held, while his other hand stroked the feathers of her chest.

"Good morning, My Lady," he said with a little trepidation. "It seems I have made one female friend in your household!"

Recovering her composure at his unexpected presence in the mews, she moved towards him and replied confidently, "Two, sir, for anyone who can make a friend of Bella Donna deserves her owner's utmost respect."

"Bella Donna? – a perfect name for this beauty. She captivated me on first sight," he said, his voice gentle as his eyes held hers.

Faye looked away as her pulse quickened, bewildered by her reaction to his gaze. Her composure quickly recovered. She related the story of Bella Donna to Ciabhan as he listened intently, the bird's head flicking from side to side, their every move in line with her vision. "She had fallen from the nest and was a sorry sight when I found her, weak and all but dead. Leon thought me mad to try to save her, but I persevered and she flourished, as you see, sir." Faye had begun to untie the cords securing her peregrine. "Would you like to hold her, My Lord? She clearly likes you," said Faye, holding the bird towards him. The Templar's breathing was heavy and she sensed a sudden discomfort as he stepped back. Given the strength that this man exuded, Faye found his reticence in wishing to hold the bird strange. "Sir?" she queried.

Struggling to find the right words, he finally stammered, "Falconry is forbidden me as a Templar."

Not knowing what to say in that moment, Faye wished she had remembered the rule. She was aware of it, but had somehow forgotten it in the tension of the moment. She could only apologise and tried to save the moment: "I, I didn't mean to embarrass you, sir." She turned to put Bella Donna back on her perch, squawking her displeasure.

"I thought I was alone," he whispered, barely audible and almost to himself. "Prior to taking the vows of a Templar, hawking had been a passion of mine," he said a little sadly.

"To see beauty in nature's gifts is not a sin, sir! God made them for our pleasure. Surely you need not take part to enjoy the spectacle?" She had felt the words to be puerile even as she spoke them, and wished she had not.

In the silence that followed she saw him closely for the first time. Although cool in the shed, his forehead was damp and a few strands of brown hair had stuck there. As he stood with lowered eyes, she noticed his eyelashes were long for a man. The shadow of them swept onto his sunburnt cheeks caught by the rising sun as it crept through a vent high on the shed's wall. His dark beard was greying, as was his hair at the temples, made darker by the oil that had been applied. The rest hung shoulder-length in untidy curls, falling onto the white Templar tunic and the linen shift beneath it. Just below the edges of the shift she saw that his skin was pale where the sun had not reached it. He was without his customary chain mail, but a short-sleeved leather jerkin exposed his nutmeg-coloured arms, the lower parts of which were criss-crossed by silver threads – battle scars from his past. Even under the dark hairs they could be seen clearly. Like moonlit paths they wound their way around his arms. She felt like tracing them with her fingertips, but banished the thought almost as soon as it had arrived.

Slowly and deliberately he lifted his arm and wrapped the leather protector securely around the bare flesh, and then, with a nod to Faye, he let her place Bella Donna upon his wrist.

Happy for him, she smiled a genuine smile for this strongest of men standing beside her gazing at the lovely peregrine.

Later that morning Faye accompanied the hawking group. The Templar spent his time with his two Turkish retainers, preferring to tilt at the quintain. He conversed easily with them in their complicated tongue. Almost imperceptibly he acknowledged her as she rode by, a smile passing fleetingly over his lips, as if lingering would somehow weaken him.

That evening, before dinner, he prayed for an hour on his knees at the high altar in the sandstone church. Absolved of sin, the Templar was agreeable company during the evening meal. Politely they spoke together, her with eyes lowered modestly and him with the utmost courtesy. Seated as the night before, Faye found herself warming to this high-principled man whose hard outer shell hid, she suspected, a soft underbelly.

The encounter in the mews was not mentioned, and neither was the leave-taking of Halbert, who had left after the morning's hunting. As he prepared to depart for his own manor he had slyly sidled up to Faye and, under the guise of taking his leave, had whispered suggestively as he bent to kiss her hand, "Such beauty, madam, is wasted here. You deserve so much more. One small yes and all I own would be yours! Think on it, my sweet, for I will not wait for ever."

She recoiled with loathing from his closeness, and snatched her hand from his. Ciabhan, watching from the crowd, had been a silent witness to this scene, and consigned to memory the unpleasant incident. Unwittingly, Halbert had made what would prove the deadliest mistake of his life.

When the time came for the Templar to leave the next day, he dutifully kissed Faye's hand and embraced Leon, thanking them both for their hospitality. Speaking directly to Leon, he said, "Your bravery in the face of battle, sir, has been exemplary, and I am in your debt. Maybe you should consider joining the Templars!" He looked towards Faye, who stared back stonily.

"No, sir! My responsibility is to be a husband – a duty I have sorely neglected of late," replied Leon, one arm draped around Faye's shoulder, and the other raised in salute. "May God go with you, my friend. Adieu, Sir Ciabhan."

Bowing low to Faye, Ciabhan bade them both goodbye. "My lady," he said as the sudden mist hid his face from view.

Together, Leon and Faye watched the small group of riders leave. They rode north towards the city of Exeter. Travelling with the Templar were his Turkish bodyguard and the handsome young page, Alain. Faye had enjoyed the company of Alain, finding his tales of Aquitaine fascinating.

As the sound of their departing diminished, Leon was the first to speak: "Well, wife, time for each other at last! We have a lot to catch up on." Playfully he patted her rear. "And a bit more, eh?"

She brushed his hand away, impatient with such haste. Straining her eyes, she looked once more into the distance, hoping for a last glimpse of the horsemen. They had disappeared, cloaked within the shroud of mist that had rolled in from the sea. No muffled hooves, no faint shouts, just a peaceful silence returned to the walled garden as fingers of fog drifted damply under the pear tree, coating the new leaves with milky pearls of moisture. . . .

The air pressure in the solar was so heavy it felt like a weight on Faye's chest. Desperate for breath, she raised herself onto her pillow and looked slowly around, her vision blurred with sleep. The door was ajar and somewhere in the stifling room a bee now buzzed frantically in its efforts to be free again. Faye's skin was hot to the touch and the cotton coverlet had somehow worked damp and rumpled beneath her body.

Gradually the memory of the night before came back. The deprivation of a night's sleep had caught her surprisingly vulnerable. Her body ached from sitting all night on a hard stool. Under her head the down pillow was soft, and she lay a little longer on the cool linen case, reluctant to leave its comfort, and closed her eyes against the brightness that seemed to flood the room.

When unable to bear the insufferable heat or the memory of the previous night any longer she slipped off the bed, relieved to feel the cold stone floor on her bare feet, and crossed to the open door. Just about to step outside, the scent of a rose caught her senses. Looking back over her shoulder, she saw on the table by her bed a perfect yellow rose.

Momentarily confused, her mind raced and her pulse quickened with the slow realisation that Ciabhan had been in her room. The heady perfume of rose mingled with his own. She should have known immediately the unseen sign of his presence. The thought of him having been so close while she had slept on unsettled Faye. Maybe he had watched her sleep or knelt and touched her face. Could she have given any clues to her dreams in his presence? Blood pounded in her temples as the thoughts filled her head.

Soon it would be their wedding day, the dream having

come full circle, and fate would have its way, unless the threat that hung over her like the sword of Damocles should break and impale her very heart. Foolishly she pushed the possibility ever farther from her mind. Filling a small flagon from her overnight pitcher, she immersed the lovely rose in its life-giving water, then, inhaling deeply the wonderful perfume, she placed it as close to her pillow as possible while her heart beat with love for her husband-to-be.

The scent of the rose wafted through the open door, even perfuming the narrow walkway that wound its way along the highest parts of the castle. In the fierce heat of mid-morning the great stones fronting the walls roasted in the sun.

"My lady." Mati's voice was breathless. "You have just missed Master Ciabhan. He came but would not wake you. Hurry – you may yet catch them."

On tiptoes, Faye pressed her flimsily clad body against the hot stones just in time to glimpse Ciabhan and Ivan as they passed side by side under the gate. Bella Donna, perched on Ciabhan's gauntlet, fluttered her feathers irritably.

Faye was minded to call but decided against doing so. Disappointed, she watched as they headed towards the steep climb that would take them to the high meadows. Just before turning into the track, Ciabhan twisted in his saddle. Even from where she stood she could see that he winced from his wounds. Shielding his eyes from the sun's glare he looked up but, blinded by the light, he did not see her frantic waving.

To his right, Ivan rode straight as a lance. The sun's glint danced off the silver buckle at his shoulder. He did not look back.

With the sounds of their departing fading, Faye stood a little longer savouring the beauty all around her, until Mati's voice again broke the silence: "Should I have woken you? You seem a little sad?" Faye stayed quiet while Mati, waiting for some sign that her mistress was not angry, fiddled with a little strand of golden hair that had escaped from under her cap. Devoted to Faye, a look of concern crossed Mati's rosy Saxon features. Never envious, she did, however, wish at times that just a little of her mistress's beauty could be hers!

"No, Mati, of course it's not your fault. I slept far longer than was intended. You did well not to wake me. Tell me, did you speak to My Lord?" She smiled at the sweet Mati.

"Oh, yes! He was concerned that maybe you were unwell, and he felt the room was a little hot. He told me to leave the door open, and I assured him that you were tired only because the warm night had made you restless."

Faye looked uneasily at Mati. "And then? Did he say more?" she questioned.

"No. He kissed you, touched your face, smiled and left."

From deep within the surrounding woodland a woodpecker hammered, its familiar sound echoing around the valley. High above the meadows a skylark sang its joyous summer song, and Faye tried to dismiss the thought of Bella Donna's talons! Very faintly she could still hear the calls of the hunting party and the yelps of the dogs; the sounds carrying on what little breeze crept over the hills from the direction of the sea.

Causing her to shiver and the fine hairs on her arms to rise, the escaping bee droned close to her ear. Pleased that the reluctant prisoner was free, she rubbed her arms. Pink already, they had changed colour in the short time she had stood on the ramparts, and her back prickled. Now she had missed the hawking party, she had hours to occupy, and last night had installed a sense of urgency in her. Today would be ideal for writing, if she were disciplined.

Back in the chamber she crossed to the carved sandalwood chest that sat in the south-facing window alcove. Mati hummed gently in the background, busying herself in the room. She stopped when Faye said, "Today, Mati, I am going to write, but outside where there is a little air. Will you help me prepare?"

From within the chest, Faye took out the manuscript.

Wrapped in softest kid and tied with a blue ribbon, it nestled between Faye's two most treasured possessions. Tattered and bloodstained, the belt she had embroidered for Ciabhan, which she kept as a constant reminder lest she ever forget all he had suffered. Tenderly she handled it, kissing the dark stains. Mati watched her mistress, remembering well the significance of the frayed remains. In contrast, the next piece of cloth couldn't have differed more: the finest golden gauze had been made by Mati into an elegant wedding gown. Tiny seed pearls adorned the high neckline and shimmered against the gold as it lay in the chest.

Mati would say often as she sewed night after night, "This is glorious with your colouring, Faye. My Lord must have imagined how you would look."

All the way from Italy Ciabhan had carried the beautiful fabric and Faye recalled his words as he laid it in her arms: "Only the very best to drape you in on our wedding day, Faye."

Lifting the parchment from its resting place, she closed the lid of the chest, sealing her treasures once more in their sandalwood nest. Carrying the bundle of papers to her escritoire, she turned to her last entry and reread the words already written. . . .

For ever imprinted on her memory was the time she had first set eyes on Ciabhan. With honesty she had written of that meeting, trying to convey onto the paper her thoughts and feelings at that time. A year had passed before their next meeting and the day of the tourney was still vivid in her mind. . . .

Mati's humming brought Faye back to the present. Still uncomfortable as could be seen by the perspiration that seemed to be pouring from her, she spoke to her maid: "Mati, I am inclined to write in the open. Under the roof thatch would be pleasant in this heat. Come, let's see if we can move this table?"

Heaving the oak table was no mean task for the two women. They finally achieved this task with such effort that they collapsed exhausted and in fits of laughter on the bed.

"The next time my fair lady wishes to take a table onto the roof, she will do so on her own," said a worn-out Mati. Then, having laid out all Faye would require, she took her leave. Touching lightly Faye's bare shoulder, she said, "I will make some cooling lemonade. But take care, My Lady, this sun is devilishly hot and I want no fainting!" She went off still chuckling to herself down the narrow flight of steps to the kitchens.

Faye heard the footsteps of her maid as she left the walkway and, lifting her head, saw the blue hem of her skirt skim the darkness of the stairway. Here under the overhanging roof thatch the little available breeze rippled through the shade and cooled Faye's hot skin. Feeling very content, Faye hunched her back and let the linen shift fall from her tawny shoulders. The freedom of bare skin heightened senses long dormant and she shivered with pleasure. Hoisting her shift above her knees, she stretched her legs into the sun and wound her loose hair into an ivory slide, sweeping it from her eyes. Thus she wrote, the flying quill filling the pages with her bitter-sweet reminiscences. . . .

On the bright late August morning of the tourney, a strong and unseasonably fresh north-westerly fluttered the banners decorating the field of entertainment, snapping and twisting the coloured silks against the azure sky. Seagulls, white as the foam, faced into the wind and hung suspended, their raucous cries filling the air.

The day had a distinct feel of autumn about it and Faye pulled her woollen cloak gladly about her as the wind tugged the cord ties fastening her hood. She checked that the jade brooch was still pinned to her shoulder; it was a gift she did not want to lose. With thanks for their hospitality, the brooch had accompanied the courteous but formal letter from the Templar inviting them to see him compete in the tournament being held at the Abbey of Torre in the month of August.

Leisurely she and Leon rode towards the field of entertainment. Only a short distance from Pagons Ton, the abbey sat back from the sea on a wide flat area of ground dotted with old oaks to give shade in the summer and shelter from winter's fury.

As they rode, the churning sea to their right sent up white horses, spraying the travellers with creamy spume. Around them a steady throng of common townsfolk headed towards the great green swathe; children, wide-eyed with sticky faces and fingers, expectantly clutched parents' hands; streamers and bunting gaily adorned carts and wagons and the unfortunate creatures that pulled them.

Occasionally, hoping to make a name for himself at the joust, a young, enthusiastic knight in full battledress and declaring his name proudly had his guard clear a path through the masses, who cheered heartily.

All around Faye and Leon an eclectic mix of vendors noisily tempted travellers with their wares from the roadside, and the air was full of the sounds and smells of people and animals on the move.

Containing her excitement had been difficult in the days leading up to the tourney. Now, with the colourful sights stretching before her, Faye turned to Leon. He had prepared with great care and sat astride his favourite mount. For days he'd cleaned and polished harness and saddle, sword buckle and belt. She looked at her husband proudly.

Dressed especially for today, he looked resplendent in midnight-blue velvet. His tunic, with gold embroidery around the neck, was caught at the waist by a thick brown belt, from which hung his fine sword and scabbard. These he'd purchased on one of his many trips abroad, bought with the proceeds earned from those he served as a mercenary. Polished to perfection, no trace of the blood that must have dripped from the blade was visible, as the hilt, inlaid with green and red bloodstone, glowed dark beneath his black cloak.

Leon surveyed the scene before him, the morning's sun lighting his strong features. Loosing the reins he removed his gloves and nonchalantly examined his hands. "Well, My Lady, the weather bodes well for this day's entertainment. I am ready for some distraction before I leave with Sir Ralf, and there should be plenty to occupy you, my sweet! Treat yourself to some trinkets. Do you see Sir Ciabhan? And where in God's name are Mati and Torr?" Standing in the stirrups, he looked back over his shoulder.

Ignoring his irritable tone, Faye scanned the teeming green in front of the abbey, her eyes seeking the red cross on the white banner of the Knights Templars amongst all the bright standards spread before her. "No, My Lord, I see him not. And don't be so harsh on Mati. She has arranged everything for your departure. Let us enjoy our last day together."

Leon grinned his most apologetic smile, leant over and took the reins of her mount. "Come, wife, I dedicate this day's pleasure to you. Methinks you are the fairest woman in Devon!"

Laughing, they spurred their horses forward and descended the last quarter-mile to the great open place, mingling with the crowds already there.

As they picked their way to the stabling, Leon asked where they might find Sir Ciabhan and the Templar faction.

A tournament marshal pointed towards the right of the abbey. "There, sir – and strong they look, I must say. Maybe they've got God on their side!" He laughed, showing a toothless mouth as he continued: "The knight, Sir Ciabhan, is something to behold!"

Following the direction the marshal was pointing in, Faye could just see, if she strained her eyes, the white banners. Turning to the grinning man, she said, "Then they are encamped near the mulberry?"

The marshal looked at her askance, then, as if to humour

her, nodded vacantly. "Aye, ma'am, the mulberry."

This did not go unmissed by Faye.

Having stood for years beside the abbey, the mulberry tree was an integral part of her childhood memories. Supported by props, the branches bled red and black berries onto the ground beneath its shade. Like little puddles of blood, the ungathered lay around the ancient tree. For years Faye had delighted in collecting the delicious fruits concealed under the leaves. She flushed, remembering that her first tryst with Leon had been within the shelter of that very tree.

"I know what you mean, my sweet. I too remember!" Leon interrupted. "The wretch was obviously an idiot!" His words were gentle as he pushed the hood from her face. "He was probably in awe of your beauty, my dear, as I am still. Now, let us find Sir Ciabhan."

Trumpets sounded a fanfare that heralded the start of the jousting. As special guests, they took their places on raised seating with an unobstructed view. War games held no appeal for Faye, but she applauded with gusto whenever the Templars excelled in their chosen combat, and she tried not to flinch at the blows.

As the knights assembled at the start, she had nearly fainted with surprise when Sir Ciabhan, riding up to the stand, had offered up the point of his lance to her and declared loud enough for all to hear, "My Lady Faye, may I have the honour of wearing your colours this day?"

In full view of all, she had to stand, and to loud cheering had placed her colours, a silken green and yellow kerchief, on the Templar's lance.

As the drums rolled, he tucked the piece of cloth into his belt, where it fluttered bravely against the brilliant white of his tunic; he bowed in the saddle and, looking directly into her eyes, snapped shut his visor.

Like a mirage, when she blinked he had gone, thundering back to the assembled knights, restless to begin. Leon smiled at his blushing wife.

She had been queen for a day when Sir Ciabhan, on

bended knee, had presented her with his winnings. Thanking him, she had promised to donate the purse to a good cause – one close to his heart.

He had smiled – his rare smile – crinkling the corners of his brown eyes. "They are yours to do with as you wish, My Lady," he had said, placing the bag of coins into her hand.

Taking leave of Faye at the close of the day's entertainments, Leon left as arranged with his overlord, Sir Ralf of Boscombe Valle, to travel to the old warrior's homeland of Normandy. The promise had been made the previous year, and this could be his final visit to the place of his birth.

Faye tried hard to curb her emotions as Leon kissed her a reluctant goodbye.

"Weep not, sweet wife. This should be but a short turn of duty, and time passes quickly. Keep lovely for me." He turned sternly to Torr, Mati's husband. "As reeve of my manor, it is your job to care for the Lady Faye. Fail to do so and you will hang!"

Torr grunted. He would do exactly as Leon demanded of him.

Oddly it was Sir Ciabhan who had voiced his doubts about the dangers of leaving a woman alone with such poor protection. "Sir, think you that it wise to leave your wife in the company of a mere serving wench and a fool – reeve or not?"

Offended to hear Mati spoke of thus, and before Leon could answer, Faye spoke out indignantly: "Husband and, with respect, Sir Ciabhan, I am no vacuous maiden! I have travelled these paths and looked after my own interests for more years than I care to remember! That I would put myself in danger is an insult to my female integrity!" Her eyes flashing warningly to both men, she continued: "Forget not that I learned survival from the absence of men – " and, in a veiled reference to them both, she added, "men who, I recall, prefer to fight for others on the far side of the world than look to their own!"

High on the castle roof the cooling shadows moved around the walls but the sun remained relentless, beating down on Faye as the words flowed, and drying as soon as written in the ferocious heat.

Faye drank deeply from the lemon drink that Mati kept refilling, and she chewed on the little pieces of lemon floating on the surface, juicy and sharp.

For a moment she rested, closing her eyes and drifting back so many months – or was it years?

The peace on the roof was broken as Mati's voice sounded from the stairwell. She stood shielding her face from the sun. "You've been here for hours. My Lord will return soon and dinner must be prepared."

Jolted from the quiet of her thoughts, Faye was irritated by the intrusion and waved Mati away with an imperious hand gesture. Regretting her action immediately, she would not forget to apologise later, but the momentum of the present was more important. Her memories, like the tide that swept daily onto the seashore in Pagons Ton, kept coming, stopping for no man. Like this tide, her memories ebbed and flowed with the recollections of that dreadful night following such a wonderful day. Just how different all might have been had they heeded the Templar's wise advice, and if she had not been left alone with just her maid and the churlish reeve for company on what was to prove a fateful evening!

Moving once more into the shifting shade, she used the time left to her that day, and began to write again, the quill scratching swiftly across the curling parchment.

For the moment she continued with happiness, her mind bursting with the memory of that extraordinary August day of the tournament.

Later would come the nightmare, of which ,thank God, she was then blissfully unaware. . . .

The way back to Pagons Ton had been uneventful. Slowly they had made their way home with the other stragglers. Copious amounts of ale had been drunk that day, and many of the late revellers were more than a little unsteady.

Faye had been in her bed only a few hours when the acrid smell of burning and Mati's screaming woke her from a deep sleep.

"My Lady! My Lady!" The door burst open and Mati nearly fell into the room.

Faye could hear running along the gallery outside her room, and other unfamiliar voices. She sat up in time to see Mati's frightened face as she was shoved brutally to the floor by a figure whose face was hidden by a heavy hood. Faye screamed at her maid as she ran to help her to her feet, "Run, Mati! Go, go save yourself! Run, Mati! Find help!" As the terrified Mati ducked under the next blow of the intruder, Faye scrambled over the bed to where Leon's sword stood, but before her hands could grab the hilt she was roughly pulled back by an iron grip around her ankles. Yelping with pain, she was yanked back across the bed and onto the floor, landing with a excruciating thump on the wooden boards.

Winded and unable to move a muscle, she tried to identify her attacker, but still she had no idea who confronted her. Helpless and vulnerable, she lay at his feet. By now two other men had entered the room and the smell of burning was stronger. Fearing the worst she could only murmur, "Show your face, brute, or, coward that you are, am I not to know my tormentor?"

His words were still muffled but unmistakable: "Patience, lady! If we don't move now, you won't be seeing any faces!"

On his command, one of them hoisted her over his shoulder and she cried out in pain as his armour cut into the flesh under her thin nightgown. The last thing she remembered was the snapping of timber, the brightness of the flames against the night sky, and the deathly quiet as if every living thing had fled.

Gradually Faye regained consciousness, remembering very little until the flashbacks began in scenes of vivid colour. Nervously she looked around her. She was on a bed in the middle of a windowless filthy room. No clues gave her prison away. Alarmed, she looked at her body, scared of what she might see. Her night shift, other than being torn and grubby, was at least in place, and she breathed a sigh of relief. Her relief was short-lived, however. She tried to move and searing pain shot through every muscle and bruised limb. Her agony only increased as feeling throbbed back into her body. Tears began to roll down sticky cheeks, dribbling onto dry lips. As she tried to wipe them on the dirty linen, despair overtook her and great sobs wracked her tender shoulders. Alone and frightened, she cried for Leon, who would have been unaware of her predicament; for Mati, who might have suffered at the hands of these vile dogs; for her servants, who had probably died or were homeless; and even for Torr, whom Leon would now surely hang in revenge for her capture, if he were not dead already.

A key sounded in the door and within seconds a shadow blocked the little light. She attempted to lift her head, for the voice was instantly familiar. She shivered. How could she have been so blind? A heavy step scraped the floor as her unseen gaoler approached and the voice, mocking, spoke: "Well, my lovely, I trust you slept well? My apologies for the lack of comfort. That is earned later!"

In the cold comfort of Warsmead, Mati and her husband, exhausted and traumatised, cowered before the imposing Sir Ciabhan. Barely disguising his contempt for the ragged pair, he demanded impatiently, "Speak up, fools! What brings you here?"

Mati bravely spoke first; Torr seemed dumbstruck: "Sir, Halbert of Boscombe Valle has taken Lady Faye!"

Shocked, Ciabhan spat his wrath at Torr, who recoiled from such fury. "God's blood! And where were you, wretch? For that traitor to take your master's wife!" With his dagger at Torr's neck, he said, "I should slit your throat now, coward!"

The unmistakable form of Halbert stood leaning on his sword. Smugly he addressed her, making no attempt at pity: "It seems, madam, that your husband cares so much that he sees fit to leave you alone – he's more of a fool than I thought!" She recoiled as he whispered close to her ear, "Be assured that I always have my way, but out of respect I have waited too long, madam! My patience wears thin! You have two days, and then I take what I want, with or without your consent!"

She scrabbled backwards as far from his loathsome presence as she could. Using the only weapon she had, she spat in his face.

Not bothering to wipe it away, he forcefully pinned her body beneath his bulk and, with one hand over her mouth, slowly untied her hands, enjoying her fear. Tightly closing her eyes she blotted out his disgusting face as she gasped for air.

His rancid breath came in bursts close to her face as he threatened, "Not now, lady. Have no fear, not now! I will take what I desire at leisure. You will have time to savour every moment!"

He had laughed when she'd found her voice: "You have a high opinion of yourself, sir! No doubt you take all you want by force, for I could imagine nothing given to such as you! Be sure I would rather take my own life!"

Suddenly deadly serious, he said, "Then you will be watched, my dear. Every minute of your day you will be watched – no privacy at all. It will be hard, I would think, for you, my lovely. I believe you will change your mind – others have!" As he left the room, he tormented her further with the words "And don't think anyone was left alive at Pagons Ton. Your little Mati – how she fought! though not half as good as you will be! Oh! How I've planned for this, Lady Faye! And your idiot husband hands you to me on a plate!"

Leaving the room, he called a guard to watch her. A pig of a man slunk in and sat grinning at her from the corner of the room. "Dinner will be brought to you. Eat well, my dear, for you will need all the strength you can find. I enjoy a woman who puts up a fight!" He slammed the door. . . .

The sun had started its slow descent, taking some of the day's heat with it. Dry splotches of ink lay over table, parchment and linen, even on her mistress's toes, observed Mati as she approached.

"Madam, is that not enough writing for today? You really should take some rest before dinner!"

Faye sighed, stretched and examined indigo fingers. "No, Mati, it is not enough! There is time before the light goes. With each chapter I remember so much more. It feels as if I'm only just beginning. There is so much more to tell; I fear stopping now." She stood up; streaks of blue on her cheeks were dark where she had brushed loose hair from her eyes. "Dear, Mati, please have patience with me. I know this obsession of mine may seem tiresome, but it is something I must do! Call me when Ciabhan returns, but for now just leave me to continue writing. There is plenty of time yet."

Mati gathered up the empty jug and cups and left with a shrug. "As you wish, My Lady."

She left Faye in peace to ponder the terror of those days held at the mercy of the vile Halbert. The frantic clicking of a blackbird's warning call brought her back to the present as it darted along the wall, wings tight across its back. She wondered what had caused its panic. . . .

Held by Halbert at the Manor of Boscombe Valle, it had taken all Faye's guile and cunning to stay one step ahead of her captor. Alternately he had used threats and promises. From being kept in filth, he then tempted her with luxury, and she was taken to a superbly furnished room. At her disposal were washing facilities, privacy, and finest linen upon which to lay her head; but strangely it was in the comfort that she felt most at risk. If her detestable gaoler were about to ravish her as threatened, she would feel a traitor to Leon here in such fine surroundings. At least in squalor there remained the chance that it might shame Halbert. She doubted, though, that he had the capacity for shame!

On the third night he came. Finely attired and highly perfumed, he had swaggered through the door. Standing in its frame he spoke: "Well, madam, I have waited long enough. These loins burn with passion. Prepare for a real man!"

She backed away.

He advanced towards her smirking, his very person revolting and reflecting all her worse nightmares. He drew his sword and laid it on the bed, then slowly unbuckled his belt. As he untied the laces on his shirt she forced her eyes from his naked torso as he sneered, "There is no escape. It really is useless to resist. Why, you may even enjoy what I have to offer here, sweet lady!"

He forced her hand roughly to his manhood as he struggled out of his breeches. With his other hand he grabbed a handful of her hair, jerking her head back until she sobbed with pain.

"God knows why of all the woman I could take, you were the only one I ever really desired; but you, madam, were too proud – too proud for me who would have given you everything!" She wilted as he raged. "God's blood, woman, what makes you so special to deny me, Halbert of Boscombe Valle?"

His body was so close that she felt violated already. Desperate, she fought rising panic as hysteria rose in her throat. Aware that time was running out, she had only cunning as a weapon. With courage she found her voice and spoke, nearly choking on the words, knowing that his eyes devoured her body beneath its flimsy night shift.

Desperate, she offered her most inviting smile. "Come, sir! a little less haste, please. This is not seemly! If I am to be ravished, please allow me a little wine." She looked up at him coyly. "It would help to relax me. It is some time since I have known great passion!"

Puzzled by her change of mind, his eyes narrowed, and he released his grip on her hair. His ardour weakened somewhat. Breathing heavily, he put his lips to her shiny locks, caressing them and whispering huskily, "A chance maybe that you could care, madam?"

She gasped, "Time will tell, sir. Patience! First it is proper to woo me."

Halbert was no fool; he saw the flicker of relief, and triumph. Savagely he pushed her onto the bed, red-faced at her trickery. "Play no games with me, mistress! Think not that I am your fool of a husband!" His passion was obvious as he tore the shift from Faye's shoulders. "I'll enjoy your screams even more now, lady."

Barely audible, the chilling swish of steel being unsheathed sounded from below. Senses tuned to the sound of combat gave Halbert precious seconds, and he lunged for his sword. Seizing Faye, he tried to make his escape – but too late! He found his way barred by Ciabhan and Alain. Confronted by his adversaries, he had no escape and he backed into the chamber, dragging Faye in front of him, one arm tight across her neck, the other gripping his sword. Hardly able to breathe, Faye wildly fought for air and clutched at her captor's arm as he taunted her would-be rescuers with vile jibes. "Well, well, Sir Ciabhan, what a surprise! The Knight Templar comes for the little whore! If her husband saw fit to leave such a catch alone, it's no great loss as I see it! So what say you, sir, to sharing this lively prize?"

Ciabhan, ignoring the sneers, fixed his opponent with the deadly stare of a predator stalking its prey. Sword in hand, he steadied his stance. Almost imperceptibly swaying from left to right, he steadied himself ready for the cut and slash of close combat. To his master's left, Alain moved stealthily inch by inch, aware that when the inevitable kill came it would be Ciabhan's alone.

His space lessening, Halbert had about him a look of desperation, and threatened, "A whore's a whore when all's said and done, but I promise to take this one with me!"

A low hissing came from Alain and Halbert's eye flicked

away from his opponents for only a second. But it was enough for Ciabhan to plunge his sword into soft flesh – Faye's flesh, as she was thrown in front of his blade.

In horror he watched as she slid to the ground while Halbert, free of his human shield, lunged. With nerves of steel, Ciabhan parried Halbert's slash, knocking his sword from his hand. On Ciabhan's second blow Halbert screamed as he succumbed in a welter of blood, the flesh between neck and shoulder split to the bone. His head hit the stone with a crack.

Just before she fell, Faye felt a shove on her back; she saw the man before her lunge and behind his eyes the anguished look as she fell onto the cold steel. Her vision dulled behind curtains of red while a tortured voice, from somewhere deep in her head, cried out, "God in heaven, no! No!"

Hooves clumping as they rhythmically thudded over the ground reached Faye's senses as she gradually regained consciousness. Her head bobbed against a tough yet yielding surface. From the smell she guessed it must be leather. The gradual dawning of where she was comforted her as she nestled in the crook of her rescuer's arm, drifting slowly between wakefulness and sleep. Her body hurt terribly and she tried not to move, frightened to disturb the comfort of her position across her liberator's lap. Her rescuer must have felt her stir.

Soothingly he spoke, and moisture from his hair dripped onto her cheeks. With rough hands he dried them with her hood, whispering as he did so, his words fading on the wind in the trees, "Stay still, My Lady. You are safe, and we are riding for the convent of the Sisters of Poverty. It is only a short way now."

She tried to speak but no words came.

Again he spoke, curtly this time: "Speak not, madam. Save your strength."

In her semi-conscious state the ride seemed interminable. When open, her eyes recognised black branches, and sometimes a bright star or two. Relentlessly the image of Halbert crashing to the ground under the onslaught of

Ciabhan's sword returned to haunt her. His body awash with blood, he lay as he had fallen, startled surprise on what remained of his face, the dreadful gaping wound oozing its river of red. The horror of that scene in the chamber was worse than the pain that threatened to engulf her. Helpless, she clung to the warmth of the man in whose arms she rested, feeling his breath on her face and the movement of his body beneath hers as he carried her to certain safety, and she let her body relax into his protecting embrace. Through misty and heavy eyes the glimmer of light got bigger and brighter until she determined it was no star but a dimly lit grill in a wall.

She heard Ciabhan's command as the horses skidded to a standstill, jolting her back to painful reality, and the rusty scraping as the grill was slowly slid aside. A woman's tired voice was cut off in mid-sentence as Ciabhan's voice, urgent now, demanded, "Open, woman. The Lady Faye of Pagons Ton needs your help! Quick, Alain, she wakes!"

Strong arms lifted her limp and breathless from the stamping steaming horse.

"She bleeds still, sir," said Alain as Ciabhan, with Faye in his arms, strode along rain-damp cloisters, closely followed by the elderly Mother Edytha. Pain flooded through Faye as she was laid on a hard bed.

Something wet trickled from her shoulder and ran down her chest with sticky warmth, gathering in a puddle under her shoulder blades. Even in a semi-conscious state, Faye recognised the feeling of blood loss and tried to raise herself.

Edytha scolded, "For pity's sake, child, stay still. This must come off!"

Obediently Faye took the liquid dribbled into her mouth, before she passed out.

Efficient and medically informed, Edytha gave instructions to her novices, who had joined her bearing hot water and clean linen bandages. Quietly they administered soothing salves to Faye's wounds. To Ciabhan, anxiously pacing, she said, "On your knees would be better, sir, for this lady is going to need all your prayers."

Free of her earthly fetters, it seemed to Faye that she hovered in limbo above the bed. Oddly, she looked down on her body. How small it appeared! and why so many in the room? Sir Ciabhan looked so sombre. She wished to flee the depressing room and fly free, but an invisible presence kept her against her will. The bright stain beneath her spread. It was curious how it matched the red cross on the watchers' tunics. On the wall over her head hung a painted Christ. Two dark marks, the colour of wine, soiled the holy hands, and blood oozed from his side, tainting it with unseen violence. Frightened, she struggled to shut out the vision of suffering, to turn from the rising tide of red. With consciousness came the pain also, filling every part of her being as she tried once again to move.

Hearing Faye's groan of agony, a relieved Edytha glanced at the knight in the corner of the room. "She has returned to us, sir. It seems your prayers have not gone unanswered."

Silently the Templar crossed himself before nodding in her direction. "Then your work is well done, Mother, and the Almighty has listened."

As Faye lay safe within the sickroom, a man's low voice in the background rose and fell in conversation. A cloth was placed on her forehead, cooling and fresh, and Faye tried to focus sticky eyes on her nurse.

Mother Edytha spoke: "My Lord, she wakes! Come, sir do not be shy. A lady should know who her champion is."

The blurred shape of a man gradually formed in front of Faye. Instinctively she knew it was not that of Leon. She tried to move her lips but no sound came.

Her distress caused Ciabhan to bend close – so close that she felt his breath on her cheek as he spoke: "Faye, you are safe here for as long as it takes. But you must rest; you have been sorely wounded."

The realisation of who her saviour was made her wish to thank him, and she fought the pain to answer him.

Stopping her, he placed a finger on her bruised mouth as she clung to his last words: "May God keep you in his care. I doubt we will meet again, but I pledge you my honour."

She sensed a ring being slipped onto her finger, then as soft as duck down on bare flesh she felt his beard brush the back of her hand.

Taking leave of the sickroom he turned to Edytha. "Make no mistake, Mother, this lady must be afforded all she requires for as long as she needs. If she comes to harm, the consequences for you will be dire."

It took more than a love-struck knight to intimidate this Mother Superior, even though his appearance was fearsome. Taking him by the arm, she said with a twinkle in her eye, "Come, sir, this has been a difficult time. Take a little wine with me before you leave."

With one last look at the tiny figure on the bed, he allowed himself to be led from the room. The crafty old woman was curious to learn the truth about this chivalrous knight and the wife of his friend, Leon, and she asked numerous questions.

Only when the Templar had drained his cup, leant forward and in no uncertain terms had said, "Enough interrogation, woman! No more words – your job is to care for the lady, no matter the cost. Her honour is paramount," did Edytha decide against further probing of this passionate knight.

Months passed and Faye languished at the Sisters of Poverty. Slowly she regained her strength, helped by the company of Mati, who had traced her mistress to the convent. Mati's husband, Torr, had escaped Ciabhan's fury, but only at the intervention of Mati. Torr was a disagreeable brute and Faye often wondered at the attraction, if any, between the two.

Time and time again, in the hope that he had learnt of her predicament, Faye wrote to Leon begging him to take her home, but with no reply. As the months went by she worried that he had been taken ill or worse.

It took all Mati's powers of persuasion to convince Faye that Leon would never abandon her. "There could be many reasons for his delay, My Lady," she had comforted. "Just be patient. Master Leon will come to take you home, but he has to rebuild one first."

Mati guessed there was very little to return to, for the house in Pagons Ton had been virtually destroyed by fire on the night Halbert of Boscombe Valle had visited. It was a miracle that she and Torr had fled the inferno, let alone made it safely to Warsmead.

Thinking constantly of ways her mistress's spirits could be lifted, Mati suggested she make a gift for her rescuer. "As a gesture of thanks, My Lady. Someone could take it to him, maybe, in the future?"

Faye considered this, and agreed, deciding on a tapestry belt. Diligently she worked, designing and embroidering delicate symbols and prayers for the wearer's safety. Backing the finished girdle with heavy linen, she wrapped it carefully, ready for the time somewhere in the future when it could be given to Sir Ciabhan.

Never idle, Faye helped with chores, delighting the novices who enjoyed having this celebrated woman amongst them. They tried encouraging her to talk of the striking knight who had saved her, supposing forbidden love and passion, but to no avail! Faye kept her own council, smiling at their eager young faces.

Discouraged by Edytha from prying too deeply into the lady's circumstances, the young women had to use all their powers of imagination to satisfy their cravings for love and romance.

'Of noble soul and carefree mind,
And heart that knew no hate,
Fair knight that would a Templar be
On these shores met his
fate. . . . .'

The story of Brother Ivan dei Romani Scuri, scholar, theologian and would-be Templar Knight.

Faye would have been happy had she known of the perfect day the two men were enjoying in the meadows. With Ciabhan's return to Compton Berry they took advantage of every moment to hunt together, the promise to do so finally fulfilled.

Content, Faye carried on writing, embracing the task she had set herself with enthusiasm, but still the tears had flowed, dropping onto the parchment and leaving smudges where she had tried to wipe them away.

To close the chapter of her abduction and rescue, it was necessary for her to recall those circumstances that had finally brought her to Compton Berry. The memory caused pain and left her mentally drained, for there were things that would remain untold, and stay for ever secret.

The air became steadily more oppressive, and she was tiring. From the bedchamber she thought she could hear the soft voice of Mati, and wondered who she might be talking to? Surely not Torr, her moronic husband. Faye had rarely seen them converse together, and when they did, Mati could hardly be civil. It was common knowledge that she had only married the bullish Torr because she had been with his child. Secretly Faye wished Mati had left him behind in Pagons Ton with Leon, who had been the only person able to tolerate his morose company.

Faye called to her maid, "Mati, who is with you?"

Cheerfully Mati's voice rang back: "I am alone, My Lady. Can I get you something?"

Faye stood for a moment, trying to feel some air on her burning skin. Her neck and shoulders were pink where the shift had slipped down, exposing tender flesh. Beneath the light linen she could feel little trickles of moisture as sweat ran down her back. Trying to concentrate on her writing, she moved her chair once more into the ever shifting shade and answered Mati: "No, thank you. I am nearly done."

Dipping the quill, she once more began to write, this time of the day that Brother Ivan first came into her life. The early memories of this meeting would at least be happy, for it was Ivan's intervention that had bought Ciabhan back to her; he had been their fateful link. . . .

Brother Ivan had entered the walled herb garden as Faye gathered bunches of rosemary. Wild autumn winds had covered the pathways with fallen leaves stripped from the oaks that hung branches over the walls. Two novices swept leaves, rustling the silence. Faye only registered the stranger's presence when the sweeping stopped and the shy girlish whispers began.

Shielding her eyes from the low sun, she saw the slight man. As the figure approached she noticed the only relief from his sombre black attire was the bronzed skin of his face, and even that was topped by a head of the blackest hair Faye had ever seen. Straight and long, it hung below the neck of his cloak and shone with the glossy blue-black of a raven's wing. She smiled to herself, remembering the villagers' nickname for him – the Raven, because of his appearance.

Bowing deeply, the self-assured young man introduced himself as Brother Ivan dei Romani Scuri! Taken aback by such familiarity in this devout setting, Faye had no time to answer before he persisted in heavily accented English: "Apologies, My Lady. I assure you I am far from being as confident as I appear. Mother Superior was keen for me to introduce myself. I did not want to look a timid fool in her illustrious presence!" Faye had not lost her sense of humour in these months, and nearly burst as he continued with a twinkle in his black eyes: "Tell me, My Lady, has the good Mother followed me? Does she check that I have obeyed her?"

Faye suppressed a smile behind her hands as she saw Edytha at the gate. With a wave to the old lady, Faye replied, "Yes, sir, she seems content. Come, tell me your name and what brings you to our door? I suspect you are not from these shores?" Gesturing to the soft kid boots that he wore: "Totally unsuitable for our volatile clime," she said. He looked down at his fashionable boots and nodded. "True, madam! I am bound for the Templar stronghold at Warsmead. These are welcome relief from those I rode in. I fear your English weather has taken its toll of my stylish Italian footwear! I was hoping that Templar funds would provide garments and boots for neophytes at Warsmead.

At the mention of Warsmead, Faye had caught her breath. She knew that Ciabhan had been headed there after leaving her at the convent. She understood now Mother Edytha's unholy haste in instigating their meeting! Recovering her poise, she spoke politely to the stranger: "Good sir, we have so few visitors here; may I ask you to take some wine with me? We should not disappoint dear Edytha. I can see she has put considerable effort into this meeting!"

He smiled back, a wide knowing smile revealing white even teeth. "Madam, it would be my pleasure to join you in some wine."

The stranger was a little older than Faye had first thought – probably in his mid- to late thirties, about ten years' younger than Leon. He told a fascinating story of his life in Rome with a mother who wished him to join the priesthood and a warrior father. Not able to satisfy them both, he had compromised and decided on the life of a Knight Templar, hoping to keep them both happy while enjoying his own chosen path. He had been weeks travelling from Italy to offer his services to the Templars at their stronghold of Warsmead. "I saw you from the guest-room window and was curious. You were obviously not one of the sisters. Edytha supposed you might take pleasure in some fresh company."

Edytha supposed quite a lot, mused Faye. According to the artful little Mother Superior, Faye and Sir Ciabhan were the love story of the century! She answered him, toying with the magnificent emerald on her hand: "You are welcome company, indeed, sir. I rarely venture beyond these walls. Hopefully it will not be long before I return to what remains of my home."

The company of this young man lifted Faye's spirits. With hesitation she told her story: the abduction by Halbert and his murder by Ciabhan, her worries for her husband's safety, and how she lived at the convent only through the benevolence of her champion.

Ivan asked if she would trust him enough to allow him to carry a message for Ciabhan, hopefully still at Warsmead.

Taking the embroidered belt, meticulously worked with coloured threads, she said, "Please give him this, but only if he will accept it. I wish not to offend. And let him know that my prayers and thoughts are with him always."

Winter that year had passed slowly, the countryside a frozen maze of snowy fields and icy streams. Cut off from passing trade the convent frugally looked after itself. Central to its survival was the constant need to fuel the fires that heated the cooking pots.

Faye kept the letter she had received from Ciabhan beneath her pillow. In the letter he had thanked her for the gift, vowing that only death would see the belt removed. He had wished her well and pledged his honour, signing it 'your devoted servant'.

Delivered by a passing monk before winter did its worst, the contents had warmed her soul on bitter nights as she huddled with the sisters in the communal dining hall. Making use of every bit of warmth, they had elected to sleep like this rather than freeze alone in the little rooms allocated them. She reread the cherished words in quiet moments, then tucked the crumpled paper back in its hiding place.

A makeshift altar in the corner of the room saved them from making trips outside, even to the chapel. Edytha had already lost two of her hardiest to the cruel winter, and was adamant that no more should succumb. "God will have to share in our hardship," she had said to the bemused novices.

February tightened winter's vice; dark and bleak, it

depressed even the most stalwart. Faye struggled bravely against her feelings of abandonment.

On a day of biting wind in April, and with no warning, Leon came for Faye. Reluctantly she left with him. Hunched against the chill they turned their mounts towards the marshy coast and home.

When Faye was to see Ciabhan and Ivan again, the pain of the meeting was to change the course of their lives forever, fate having woven finally its own threads of destiny. . . .

After farewells to Faye and Edytha, Ivan had made his way to Warsmead. Arduous weather conditions made the going unpleasant. He pondered the plight of the lady left at the convent.

At one inn stop he studied the belt entrusted to his care. Examining it carefully he wondered at the significance of the delicate symbols. Exquisite in their detail, the colours glowed in the candlelight. Were they coded passionate memories? A deep romantic spark in him imagined they were! A prayer of thanks preceded blue waves framing a red church and a small house. A falcon sat atop two enjoined hands, with a dazzling green ring in its hooked beak. Was this the ring he had seen on the finger of Lady Faye? Encircled by white banners with their red crosses, a green field of tourney stretched in front of an abbey. Oak leaves and acorns entwined with mulberry fruits of the deepest ruby ran the length of the belt, while Anglo-Saxon and Latin inscriptions for peace and love linked the little scenes. Words known only to the wearer and giver stumped him with their secret meanings. To finish, a prayer of the utmost poignancy for the wearer's safety joined the first prayer where the ties laced the two ends together. Just before the prayer, dark drops of crimson dripped from the blade of a broadsword, forming a heart in a vivid pool at its point.

Ivan held the girdle, feeling its power in the unspoken words, the linking of the paths of two people unknown to him. He was certain of one thing: he would rather die before he gave this to any but Sir Ciabhan of Compton Berry.

On a windswept hill the stronghold of Warsmead sat forbiddingly in the winter gloom. Ivan thought he had never seen such an uninviting place as he rode cold and hungry up to the door of the citadel. Hammering on the bolted door he mumbled into his neck, "Everything I ever heard about this infernal country is true." Ready to drop, he thought of the comfort of a hard pallet. Compared to the basic sleeping arrangements he'd enjoyed so far, it would be luxury.

The door creaked open, letting out welcome heat, and Ivan was greeted warmly. The young monks, eager for news of fellow knights and friends, talked enthusiastically, their enquiring minds absorbing all they could of the life they had relinquished in exchange for the battles of God.

The handsome knight entered the hall and all eyes turned. Ivan knew immediately whose presence he was in; the hushed respect that greeted Sir Ciabhan of Compton Berry was palpable. When introduced to Ivan, he courteously returned Ivan's salutation then, graciously acknowledging them all, he silently took his place amongst the younger knights at the communal trestles.

Ivan observed him from under lowered eyes. Dressed simply in a rough woollen tunic, this Templar stood out even in the company of fine knights. Most were young; he was not, but Ivan put him in his late forties. A few elders sat apart by virtue of their seniority.

A cheerful knight, sitting beside Ivan, said civilly, "I am Alain Rousseau, originally from the Duchy of Aquitaine, now companion to Sir Ciabhan of Compton Berry. I am pleased to be of service to you, sir."

Ivan carefully replied, "Sir Ciabhan appears a very fine knight, sir!"

"The very best. He is a knight extraordinaire, and I am proud to be leaving with him for France the day after tomorrow." As an afterthought, he added hesitantly, "I will be glad to leave here. My Lord has suffered indignities enough at the hands of Warsmead's Grand Master!"

Ivan again looked over at Sir Ciabhan. Finished with eating, Ciabhan was preparing to leave the table. He drained his cup and stood. Each and every knight present rose and stood until he had left the room – all except one, the Grand Master, who sat alone as the elders stood. The Grand Master followed the exit of Sir Ciabhan of Compton Berry with malice written on his flaccid features. Resignedly he appeared to accept his defeat and placed his knife, still with its portion of meat, deliberately on the table.

Ivan caught Alain's attention again; if he was to initiate a meeting with Sir Ciabhan he had to act quickly. "Pardon my impertinence, sir, but I have a matter of some urgency that may be of interest to your master, if an opportune moment could be found? I come from Devon where I broke my journey for a while at the convent of the Sisters of Poverty!"

Alain thought awhile then said, "After Mass tonight – his room."

Shown into the round chamber, whose door remained open at all times, Ivan was surprised by its sparseness. Air filtered through a small opening high on the wall. Light from a candle flame danced on the crucifix that hung on the wall above the altar, whose only concession to decoration was the red and white banner that served as an altar cloth. Another banner hung above the bed – a small hard pallet, coverless except for a thin blanket, neatly folded. The room was cold, the whole atmosphere being one of deprivation and penitence. No table or stool gave homely comfort. Quite simply, this was the room of a man of war, with only the bare minimum of requirements. Most of the remaining space was taken up by the clothes and accoutrements of battle. Lance, sword and dagger rested against the wall, gleaming as the weak light from a tiny candle flame bravely danced upon polished surfaces. A suit of chain mail hung from its stand, belt and scabbard across the shoulder. On another stand was draped the pristine white tunic with its red Templar cross.

Ivan touched the coarse linen, recoiling as he remembered the vivid stories told by his father of the horrors of war. He imagined this very tunic reddening with the wearer's blood.

Behind him a voice spoke: "So, sir, I believe you have something of importance for me?" Lost in his thoughts, Ivan jumped as Sir Ciabhan continued: "Alain said you wished to speak to me, so speak up, sir, my time is short!"

Reaching into his cloak, Ivan pulled out the bundle and gave it to the Templar. "I was entrusted to give this to Sir Ciabhan of Compton Berry, should I have the opportunity," said Ivan, slightly in awe of this commanding knight.

"And who would ask such a task of you?" said Ciabhan, looking directly at Ivan as first he examined, then opened, the package.

"A lady," replied Ivan. "A very lovely lady!" he added, watching the change in Ciabhan's expression. For minutes Ciabhan gazed speechless at the gift in his hands, and Ivan spoke quickly: "It was not her intention to offend, sir!"

Ciabhan studied intently the symbols, their meaning so clear to him. Slowly, he unrolled the belt to its full length, reading with great care the prayer at its end. "She could never offend me, sir!" With the faintest smile the Templar addressed Ivan. "This is a rare gift indeed, and I thank you for your trouble."

In that small room by the light of the struggling candle, Sir Ciabhan stripped naked and, with great care, fastened the girdle around his middle. Ivan watched as he patiently laced the green-and-gold ties, securing the ends meticulously with a double knot while his chestnut hair fell over strong shoulders.

When finished, he raised dark eyes to Ivan and said passionately, "Only death and all its demons shall part my body from this belt. Mark you well these words, Alain!"

"I understand, My Lord," the young knight replied,

helping his master back into his simple shift.

The Templar's next words showed just a chink in this powerful man's armour as he enquired of Ivan almost tenderly, "And fares my lady well? Does she enjoy good health? Know you in truth, sir, that never have I left one so reluctantly!"

Ivan recounted to him the story Edytha had told of the lovers' harrowing flight from Boscombe Valle after the murder of Halbert. He added that, in his conversation with her, Faye had shown concern only for the welfare of the valiant Templar, emphasising that her prayers were for him.

In the gallery the two men sat talking on a low bench while Alain organised arms in the chilly round room. Ivan explained the reasons for him being at Warsmead and his dreams of becoming a Knight Templar, from where best he could serve God and Christianity. Their combined knowledge of languages made conversation between the two men easy. Both were highly intelligent and well travelled. Each au fait with spiritual life, they had much in common. Respect for each other grew even in that short period. Not once, however, did the Templar mention again the lady whose token of gratitude he now wore tight about his waist, although frequently he felt that the belt was in place.

"Well, Ivan dei Romani Scuri," he had said warmly clasping Ivan's hand, "now to rest. Tomorrow I take a journey of atonement. I think I will not set eyes on these shores again. Think very hard on the life you choose, sir!"

Sleep eluded Ivan that night. Physically exhausted, his mind would not let him rest. Pulling his cloak over his head, he walked to the window and looked into the cold night sky. A multitude of stars flooded the immense black void; Orion, the great hunter, strode across the darkness. Many a night in this inhospitable land Ivan had lain down in some makeshift shelter, falling asleep under the hunter's watchful presence. He shivered – tonight had a magical feel! From above his head an owl hooted, and its invisible mate answered that melancholy call from the emptiness. 'Another hunter,' Ivan thought. This night seemed to speak to him! Something strangely mystical was confusing his mind; silence thundered around him and the brilliant stars drew him into their midst. 'Follow the hunter,' they pleaded.

Apparent at last, Ivan understood: Ciabhan was Orion! He was to follow the Templar! To the echo of the owls he finally fell into a satisfied sleep, his mind made up.

In the cold pre-dawn he found Sir Ciabhan alone in the chapel on his knees before the altar. Aware that someone had entered, the knight genuflected, kissed the altar and slowly rose. His features, although careworn, had the serenity of acceptance written over them; he was a man as yet still in control of his own destiny. He smiled knowingly and spoke first: "The peace of silent and black night can often clear our minds, sir! Is it not so?"

Ivan smiled back, amazed at the Templar's perception, and he held out his hand in friendship. "It appears so, my friend. I would be honoured to accompany you, if you would have me? It seems the hand of providence has linked the paths of our lives, the purpose of which we have yet to discover."

Such a hasty decision meant a slight setback: horses, baggage and supplies had to be found.

Ivan was introduced to his fellow companions. Alain he already knew, but not the two dark Turks who were the Templar's personal escort. As expected, he was clothed and armed courtesy of the foundation; money he had of his own. Alongside Alain on a new horse, and without a backward glance, he rode out from the Temple of Warsmead.

Death, in all its disguises, constantly stalked the knights who fought for Christianity in the hot and inhospitable lands of the heathen. If an arrow, lance or scimitar failed to end a life, then the bloody flux or some other foul disease would do so, coupled with all the indignities it could heap upon already desperate flesh. A varied diet, when possible, and plenty of clean water was known to aid the body in fighting infection, and Ciabhan was expert in keeping his men safe. Whether in battle or at peace, his fellow knights' well-being was a priority.

Taking succour from Christian charities, the small band of five, as well as three pages that looked after armour and supplies, made their way uneventfully to the Holy Land. Once arrived, they joined other groups of crusaders, all seeking vain glory in the name of the Christian God. Occasional skirmishes fuelled their enthusiasm for battle and gave welcome practice for combat. Never in one place for long, they formed a close and tight-knit unit.

Ciabhan was a hard taskmaster and exacted a standard of behaviour that befitted his social standing. Merciless in battle, his admiration for valour, however, showed no prejudice; friend and foe earned his respect for courage.

Because of this, the little group enjoyed an enviable reputation as their fame grew. Ivan surprised the Turks by learning some of their difficult language and taking the trouble to understand the differences between their cultures.

From their first meeting, Ivan and Ciabhan had been kindred souls; both had tremendous physical strength combined with the mentality of fighting men. Ivan's natural gentleness was the perfect foil for Ciabhan's impatience – especially with fools. In the soft glow of campfires, wrapped against the desert chill and fuelled by warm wine, they would pit their wits against each other in the game of chess, pushing the boundaries of strategy and arguing the logic of reasoning.

At times, Ivan would scold his intense opponent: "Shame on you, sir! That is not a gallant move!"

Ciabhan's face, harsh in the dancing flames, would reply bitterly, "My back bears the scars of chivalry, my friend! And my soul burns still with its consequences! The queen only is sacred! No mercy for bishop or king – they are all forfeit!"

It was under the incandescent canopy of desert stars, during these games of chess, that little by little Ivan learned just how much Ciabhan had suffered for the rescue of the Lady Faye. There was also a slow realisation that, although never actually admitting it, this strong knight, regardless of his religious vows, was totally enamoured of his friend Leon's wife! Ciabhan remained reluctant to discuss an incident that he considered personal.

Any information came mostly from Alain, who had accompanied Ciabhan on that fateful night. He spoke openly to Ivan. "Sir Ciabhan has suffered humiliation, more than one of his standing should have to," he said. "He accepted absolutely the punishment given and has rarely spoken of it. But surely a flogging in the presence of Templar brothers who were forced to watch is a punishment too far. What worth a knight if he is unable to protect the honour of a fellow knight's wife in the absence of her husband? It makes a mockery of chivalry! What say you, Brother?" Not waiting for a reply, he carried on talking and it was obvious that the indignities heaped upon Ciabhan provoked a passionate response from the young man. "Have you seen the lash marks on my lord's back? Discipline, the Grand Master called it! But I was not alone in seeing his smile of satisfaction as the blood flowed. He's a monster of a man – petty and riddled with jealousy over Ciabhan's fame. That was the real reason!"

Alain's disgust was obvious. It had not escaped Ivan's notice that the Grand Master at Warsmead was of a cruel and vindictive nature, and he answered Alain truthfully: "Well, Alain, what I witnessed in my short time at Warsmead changed my opinion on committing to the order. As you are aware, I made a decision to follow Sir Ciabhan after my visit there – a choice not made lightly. Yes, it was wrong to treat such a man so, for, in the little time I have been acquainted with Sir Ciabhan, I have come to know a man of extreme honour. A truer knight of Christendom does not exist." Trying to reassure the young man, Ivan talked freely. "God moves in mysterious ways.

If we were in control of our destinies, think you we would fare any better, Alain? It is not for us to question His great plan. I could now be back at Warsmead and not dying of thirst in these godforsaken hills!"

Ivan threw his arm around Alain's shoulder as they walked past the Turkish bodyguards, who, polishing their murderous weapons in the sun, smiled, white teeth gleaming in aquiline faces. "Thank the Lord those two are Christian and on our side," Ivan said light-heartedly. Ivan liked the young man who had confided so much in him.

Tall and muscular, the young knight from Aquitaine had started service in the pay of Ciabhan as a page. Now twenty-five he was as close to his master as a son would be. Fresh-faced with a wispy beard and dark-blue eyes, he was fired with the enthusiasm of youth.

Ivan hated seeing him angry or sad. "Come, let us find some refreshment," he said.

But Alain, earnest again, turned to Ivan and asked, "Tell me, Brother, has fate changed your course so greatly?"

Ivan thought on the ways of destiny before answering. "In Rome I studied theology and the priesthood for my mother, and warfare for my father. In dreams I sought to challenge the world with new and profound ideas! To date I have changed nothing but my mind! It is God's plan that I am here, and I must accept it."

On one spectacular night, as heaven's beauty enfolded them in its cool embrace, Ciabhan and Ivan were playing a particularly tense game.

Ivan said matter-of-factly, "It was gracious of you to write to the Lady Faye before we left the shores of England, sir. It would have been a comfort at least for her to know that the gift was pleasing to you."

Ciabhan, absorbed in his move, replied without looking up, surprising Ivan with his frankness: "It is no comfort to me that the lady doubtless lies in her husband's arms as we speak! My torment goes on!" Taking advantage of Ivan's momentary lack of concentration, he slammed into his next move, clearing the board. With eyes glittering almost as brightly as the stars themselves, he pronounced triumphantly, "Your move, sir?"

That was the nearest Ciabhan had come to mentioning Faye, and it was weeks before he spoke of her again.

Small signs, however, gave away the truth. The colours green and gold appeared to have some significance; two small silk ribbons fluttered from Ciabhan's lance at all times, now bloody from battle. Meticulous in making sure they were secured, he said they were a reminder of England's spring green and autumn amber. On airless nights in uneasy dreams, when sleep was slow in coming, Ivan would watch as Ciabhan's hands sought the girdle around his waist, and he noticed how it gave him comfort.

While Ciabhan suffered for whatever sins assailed him, Ivan's curiosity was stirred more and more by the story he'd heard while in Devon. He smiled, recalling the ploys of Edytha as she'd succeeded in getting him to meet with Faye. Many a night, disturbed by Ciabhan's restlessness, he would lie awake, the thoughts turning in his mind: the appalling Halbert, and why Leon would leave his wife alone so long. Was there real cause for jealousy, or was it all a tragic misunderstanding? Ciabhan was a leader and not given to making irresponsible decisions. He lived by a code of honour, but honour should not result in a flogging. Ivan had seen the raw red stripes, first at Warsmead, as Alain had fastened the belt for him. The sight had shocked him. With so many whys, it was a relief when the lulling sounds of the settling camp would finally bring welcome sleep.

It was after one such night of little sleep for Ivan that the group ran headlong into an ambush the next day. Unprepared for the speed and ferocity of the attack, Ciabhan was particularly hard on himself. "God's blood, I should have seen that coming!" he cursed. "There can be no excuse."

Alain, the least wounded, offered some consolation: "They all perished, sir! Not one survived. That's seven heathen dogs less!"

Ciabhan grimaced as he tried to cleanse the deep slash

in his side, reminding them both, "Never underestimate or trust the armies of Allah, my friends. An enemy that smiles equally while drinking tea or slitting your throat is clever, charming and devilishly cunning!"

The ambush had been bloody, with not one of Ciabhan's party escaping without some injury. Fiercely they had fought side by side until their swords were drenched in the blood of the dead assassins. The traitorous wretch who had led them into the trap lost his head in one slice from a Turkish scimitar while begging in vain for mercy.

Nursing bloody wounds back at camp, Ciabhan blamed himself for trusting the scout, and raged, "By the bones of Christ! how often have I warned against trusting these dogs? I could have got us all killed, fool that I am!"

Alain, frustrated by Ciabhan's bad temper spoke up: "Will you be still, sir. Blaming yourself is ill-founded, for the day has been won!"

Ciabhan grumbled a little more as Alain poured alcohol on the wound, and then he cursed!

Ivan sighed heavily and considered the sorry group of bruised and bloody men. Alain was the only one amongst them who was not disabled by his injuries, and staunchly he attended to their needs. He organised pitchers of clean water, and bathed and dressed gashes with the patience of a saint. Ivan's head throbbed and a lump the size of an egg rose at the back where the hilt of a sword had clubbed him, breaking skin but not the bone. He struggled to focus on the scene around him as his vision doubled, watching as a fuzzy Alain tried to remove the belt from Ciabhan's waist.

Ciabhan, grasping it tightly, refused to cooperate. "Curse you, it's only a scratch, man!" he scolded. "The belt remains where it is!"

Sensing Alain's irritation with Ciabhan's stubbornness, Ivan said, "Leave it, Alain – he will survive! The others need you."

Ivan realised that in this climate such a serious injury would quickly fester and cause complications. He staggered to Ciabhan, and, without drawing attention to his action, he discreetly looked beneath the belt. He knew the girdle was best left where it was, holding the bleeding wound together.

Deep red, the blood seeped, slowly discolouring and stiffening the white tunic – the very tunic he had seen hanging in the chamber at Warsmead. A chill shuddered through Ivan at the memory, for like a vision clearly forecast was the very scene he had pictured in his mind, and he prayed for his friend.

For all Ivan's careful tending, Ciabhan failed to improve as quickly as hoped; his pain was obvious as the healing process dragged on slowly. Unable to ride out, his days were spent resting in the coolest shade available, listening to the tales of others – a pastime that frustrated such an active man.

One searingly hot afternoon, Ivan sipped sweet tea with a despondent Ciabhan. Struggling to cheer him with details of their latest successful skirmish, he made light conversation as the life of the camp played out noisily around them. Braying asses, bad-tempered camels and nimble goats contributed to the cacophony of sound assailing their ears.

Beneath the relative privacy of a colourful awning, the petty squabble of two herders jarred the nerves as Ivan informed Ciabhan of a decision he had made. "This climate is not aiding your recovery, Ciabhan. I am of a mind to retire to Sicily. The air is more agreeable and the doctors are skilled in this type of injury." Swatting away the swarms of mosquitoes gathered for attack, he waited for Ciabhan's reaction.

"Do what you must, Brother. I am in your hands," he said wearily, closing his eyes.

Ivan continued, surprised at his friend's lack of protest: "I'll make arrangements as soon as possible. When fully recovered, maybe we can make the crossing to Rome? She lies only a short distance from Sicily." He looked to Ciabhan, expecting a reply, but he was already in deep sleep.

Ivan called one of the quieter boys nearby to stay and fan the flies from his friend. "Keep him cool, lad, and the bugs away! There's a coin or two for your time." He pressed some coins into the sticky palm of the beaming boy.

It was crucial that Ciabhan be moved as soon as possible, so, on an unusually grey morning, but in good spirits, the little group sailed from the dusty shores, leaving behind the deprivations of campaigning for the softer climes of Sicily. There they could lick their wounds in the comparative safety of a Christian country, where the fear of an assassin's arrow would not dominate every waking moment. In fertile plains the challenges of conflict could be exchanged for healing respite, whether Ciabhan liked it or not.

Alone on the high deck of the fast vessel, with Ciabhan comfortably settled under cover, Ivan faced the wind. The force of the wind pulled his hair into a stream behind him and whipped at his cloak, pulling the fabric tight across a body muscled and strong from months of hardship and exertion. He inhaled deeply. Leaving the land of heady spices, he was certain he could smell already the perfume of orange and lemon cutting through the breeze. As the spray wet his face, he marvelled at the forces of nature and the power of the sea, holding it in great respect. Never a lover of things marine, he used the sea only when unavoidable as a means of transport.

Now, as the ship plunged westwards, he thought suddenly of England for the first time since leaving its green shores so long ago. Was it the hard and unrelenting sand and ochre shades of the Holy Land that, for a fleeting minute, made him yearn for that shrouded land with its chill mists of green and grey? Maybe it was the months he had endured on barren ground – the longing for sight of a tree in full green leaf, or dew as it lay in droplets on soft moss! Of one thing he was certain: at this moment he had no desire to ever set foot on desert soil again!

Ciabhan's self-sacrifice had been admirable, but surely his atonement was complete. If Ivan had helped liberate his friend from, as Ivan saw it, the ongoing unnecessary penance, then he was a happy man. Enough was enough, and the debt was paid! Although wealthy men in their own right, both had chosen to lead prudent and frugal lives, one whilst fighting in the name of God for his Christian beliefs, the other on a journey of personal discovery, testing his own beliefs.

The weather warmed the further west they ploughed, and Ivan felt at peace, knowing the decision he had made had been the right one. He was totally unprepared for the vision of Faye that suddenly flashed into his mind. Strangely disconcerted, he turned and looked down the length of the boat, almost as if expecting to see her coming towards him. Simultaneously, Ciabhan, from inside the leather shelter, raised his hand weakly and smiled at his friend.

Sicily afforded them the sanctuary they needed. On the top of a hill rising from a flat plain, the Templar-friendly fortress gave them welcome succour whilst licking their wounds. It also allowed the combat-weary group a chance to clear battle-clouded minds and to see a horizon that stretched beyond the next clash.

Isolated, the citadel was a haven of peace and tranquillity. Ciabhan had improved. The wound, although slow in healing, had finally knit together in a jagged scar that pulled with the slightest physical exertion, causing him to catch his breath.

One sultry afternoon, as he lounged with Ivan beneath a vine heavy with its purple harvest, Ciabhan gave the first indication of his intentions: "My friend, at times I long for the green of England. For too long I have neglected Compton Berry."

Ivan, lazily stuffing succulent green olives into his mouth, listened and then said, "By God, these are good! Do not forget that you have been unwell, Ciabhan. When fit, of course you shall return! It was not choice but necessity that brought us here. So have patience. We will see the winter out here."

Ciabhan laughed at his friend. "You fuss too much, Brother. I am no weak woman, and this inactivity bores me!"

Goat-bells tinkled from far below the fortress walls; the sound rising and falling as the wearers grazed on sparse grass in the shade of stubby citrus groves. With an effort, Ciabhan pulled himself up and strolled to the wall, shielding his eyes as an eagle called. Soaring above them, it flapped its great wings languidly in the cloudless blue ether, scanning the ground for prey. Ciabhan shivered involuntarily and Ivan noticed beads of sweat on his friend's brow, although his skin was like ivory.

"It is for your sake that I wish you fully recovered. You still have some way to go," said Ivan.

Ciabhan nodded impatiently, the moisture flicking from the ends of his hair. "I know," he said, straining to follow the huge bird as it flew from sight. "I know, my friend, but how I wish I were that eagle with wings to bear me home!"

The speed and severity with which Ciabhan succumbed to the fever could not have been foreseen. It struck without warning a body already weakened.

Ivan remained untouched. Probably the illness was one he had been in contact with while growing up in the enclosed and stifling city of Rome – how it baked in the summer months!

Sure of his immunity, he knew no fear when caring for his comrades. Alain and one of the Turks suffered the bloody flux, but both made full recoveries, thanks to Ivan.

Ciabhan's determination to return to England grew steadily into an obsession, and nothing Ivan said would change his mind. His obduracy persisted as he continued: "You make excuses, my friend! There are men here who will risk everything for a few gold coins; the sea holds no terrors for them!

Ivan's patience was wearing thin as he replied, fighting Ciabhan's iron will with equal stubbornness, "You know it would be madness to attempt such a journey in your condition. Wait until the sickness has done with you well and truly! I beg you, Ciabhan, see sense and reconsider. Do not risk your life further!"

Angry and inflexible, they faced each other, neither giving way until Ciabhan spoke: "Mark my words well, Ivan. If I am to die, I die on English soil. My mind is made up and God himself will not change it! Now let that be an end to it!" He hesitated before adding, "All I hold dear is in that fair island. I was a fool to run from it. Tomorrow I and the others sail, with or without you!"

Fighting his rising anger, Ivan studied his friend's face. The constant pain of the last months had wreaked havoc on his handsome features; the dark-brown eyes were heavy and unnaturally bright, as if something in his spirit was broken. He returned Ivan's look defiantly, and it was quite obvious that he would have his way.

Accepting defeat, Ivan looked to the heavens as if for divine guidance. Ciabhan, with all credit, did not have the malice or spite to gloat, but said instead, a small spark in his eyes for the first time in days, "I promise you, my friend, we will hunt together at Compton Berry yet!"

In the high meadows Ciabhan and Ivan leant against the gnarled bark of a shady oak and surveyed the landscape around them. Ciabhan struggled out of his leather jerkin and wiped the sweat from his face with the hem of his shirt. Where the sweat irritated his back he wriggled against the trunk.

"By God! it's hot," he said, sweeping the damp hair from his sunburnt forehead.

Ivan agreed. "Aye," he said, equally uncomfortable, as his head tried to find a resting place against the tree. "It's hot, 'tis true, but it's not the stinking hell we endured in Acre. I think we are in danger of becoming soft in this pleasant land!"

Their laughter rang down the valley, where it mingled with the mewling and calling of the hawks as they flew, the tinkling of their jesses carrying for miles.

As they shared a flask of water, there seemed no sign of the previous night's tension, and Ivan appeared free of whatever had ailed him.

"I would not want it any other way, my friend – you by my side and an impending marriage. I need nothing more." Content with his life, Ciabhan reflected on this moment. No longer a hot-headed young man, his passion for the cause burnt less brightly. His scars hurt; this morning, twisting in the saddle to try to see Faye, his side had pulled painfully and a trickle of blood now stained his white shirt. He thought of Faye asleep this morning: little drops of moisture wet her forehead, and her eyes flickered rapidly beneath the long lashes. In the damp tangle of her hair the golden cross he had given her lay gleaming, the chain heavy across her throat, close to the little pulse spot that throbbed rhythmically with every breath she took. Not wishing to disturb her, he had left quietly, leaving a yellow rose near her pillow. Acknowledging Mati, he had said, "Leave the door open a little, mistress. The room is very hot; there needs to be some air in here." Leaving the room, he remembered Faye's maid smiling at him shyly.

From where they leant the cobalt sky gradually changed to palest blue as it touched the edge of the sea, misting as sea and horizon became one. The heat rose from the parched land as if off the back of some great sleeping beast. On a day such as this it was hard to imagine these same hills and valleys scoured by winter's wrath.

The two men sat silently for a while, absorbing the peace, until Ciabhan spoke: "It is a perfect day, my friend. God favours us."

Ivan agreed as he offered Ciabhan the flask of water. "It's perfect, except for that she-devil on your wrist!"

Bella Donna swivelled her head at the sound of his voice – or was it the sweet song of a skylark that caught her attention as it rose from the valley they had just left. She strained at her jesses.

In silence they absorbed the skylark's melody. Refreshed, Ivan was the first to rise. He stretched his slim and still supple body; age seemed in no hurry to reach Brother Ivan, thought Ciabhan.

Both wore the silver tracery of scars, but they were more prominent on Ivan's brown skin and he wore them with pride for all had been acquired in the service of Ciabhan. The legacy of one blow had left him prone to the occasional head pain, when he would shut himself away for hours.

The two seasoned warriors had certainly earned their respite. Ciabhan held out his hand to his friend. "Come, Brother, give me your hand. These joints no longer serve me quite as well!"

Ivan smiled down at the man he venerated. "That makes two of us, my friend, and I am ten years younger!"

They clasped each other, laughing. It had not escaped his notice, however, that Ciabhan had hastily gathered his jerkin about him to hide the patch of blood staining his shirt.

As they walked down the hill, Ciabhan removed the hood from Bella Donna and she launched herself from his arm, the force leaving the nerves tingling. Within moments an unfortunate wood pigeon was plummeting earthwards, her feathers floating slowly, dreamlike around the two men.

Ciabhan looked back towards the sheltering oak, its branches silhouetted against the azure sky. The song of the skylark in the valley stopped abruptly, while the flicker of a frown crossed Ciabhan's forehead.

Comradeship, forged in iron, bound Ciabhan and Ivan; it was a bond that nothing, it seemed, could break. They were two strong men whose paths had been joined by destiny, and now on this hazy summer's day they reminisced.

Ciabhan, not normally given to exuberance, threw open his arms. "I ask you, Ivan, can heaven be any better than this perfect day? What man could want more? In truth, my friend, there were times when my faith was sorely shaken, but now I give thanks to God every day for the life he gave back to me!"

"God, sir, gave you Faye. It was she who nursed you back to health," said Ivan darkly. "Do you think she would have let you go? She fought with every breath for your survival. In truth, I think she would have died for love of you. Not once did she leave your side until ill herself; then my worries doubled!"

He smiled now, but the memories of that dreadful time were still fresh in his mind. Ivan thought of himself and Faye bent over Ciabhan's broken body.

Together they had cut off the embroidered belt, so lovingly worked by her own hands, soaked in Ciabhan's blood. The frayed cloth, holding the wound together, fell into fragments, the fresh blood pouring as it was removed. Desperate, they fought to staunch the flow with astringents and white linen. Ivan recalled how dark Ciabhan's lifeblood was and how quickly it reddened the cloth. To this day he found it different to anything ever encountered on the battlefield.

The image of Faye's hair and face smeared with Ciabhan's blood, unreal and trancelike, haunted him still, replaying itself in slow motion. It was during those terrible hours, fighting for the life of the man they loved, that Ivan's respect for Faye grew. This was the woman for whom Ciabhan had been prepared to die. For the first time he began to understand the nature of love. When he had borne her gift of the belt to Ciabhan, had he been God's emissary in the great scheme of things? Fate (or was it God?) drove a hard bargain, he mused.

Later, as the countryside settled itself uneasily for the coming storm, the two friends made their way home along the rutted tracks. Wildlife teemed in the hedgerows, hiding beneath leaves thick with dust from lack of rain. Steam rising from the horses clogged the air with grime, and it settled on the sticky clothes of the riders.

Hungry and in good humour the party wound its way leisurely back to Compton Berry. Ciabhan and Ivan bought up the rear. Relaxed, they rode side by side pleased with the day's pursuits. Easily they conversed, recounting the twists and turns of fate that had linked their paths.

Ciabhan spoke unusually profoundly: "How stealthily love stalks our very souls, Ivan! I have much to thank you for."

Ivan's answer matched the rather intense statement: "If the mighty can be humbled by love, my friend, why should you be any different?"

Ciabhan looked sideways at his friend. "The wise raven speaks." Their eyes met. "And, as usual, you are right!" laughed Ciabhan as he spurred his mount ahead of his friend.

Choking in the dust, Ivan pulled his cravat across his mouth, but not before yelling, "You will pay heavily for that!" Then he smiled indulgently. Watching his friend so full of high spirits made Ivan content, but the secret he had tried to confess but had not had the courage to admit tormented him still!

As the others raced ahead, Ivan slowed to a lazy pace enjoying the lovely countryside. He noticed that Lupo had limped back to walk beside him. Ivan's thoughts drifted back to the sea voyage from Sicily; with all the odds stacked against them they had survived to return to Compton Berry where Ciabhan had lain so ill. Of course Ciabhan remembered little of the journey, being only semi-conscious most of the time.

As the first rumbles of the coming storm churned the heavy atmosphere, his thoughts returned to that nightmare passage. . . .

Weeks at sea had tested the fortitude of the tough little crew to the utmost. Exhausted and irritable they crossed the southern English Channel. Tempers were at an all-time low as they navigated the difficult entry into the mouth of the Dart. Angry exchanges over the slightest disagreements had tested all Ivan's powers of diplomacy to the limit, but ultimately the crew had gelled and done as promised; they had earned their promised gold.

On deck Ivan squinted through driving rain to see the outline of the twin fortresses that guarded both sides of the approach. Thick wooded slopes dipped to the sea, the grey forbidding cliffs indistinguishable from the waves as they surged and broke against the dark land mass. Flecks of white spume broke free of the swell, floated in the salty spray, then vanished midway between sea and sky. Seabirds, suspended in the air, disappeared into troughs then reappeared over the crests.

Sensing the end of their marathon voyage, the oarsmen pulled hard into the river's mouth, its waters benign in comparison to the open sea they had just left. The tide was in their favour and carried the relieved group steadily upstream, the river twisting its way past thick overhangs not yet clothed in spring's glory. Glimpses of red soil from the steep banks gave warmth to the landscape that peeped through the trees. These were the colours that Ivan remembered from his first visit to Devon. Herons in the shallows moved not a feather as the ripples from the oars fanned out and broke sluggishly against skinny legs.

Ivan's moment of quiet was suddenly broken by Alain's frantic calling. "My Lord, come quickly!" The young knight's voice bought Ivan to his side. "It's Ciabhan – he will not settle. I fear for him!" said Alain.

Under housing on the deck, Ciabhan lay on a makeshift bed. In the fetid cabin covers were strewn around, stiff with sea water and soiled with vomit. Struggling to raise himself, Ciabhan threshed upon his pallet as Alain tried to restrain him.

Opening a package he carried, Ivan held the opiate to his friend's parched lips. "Come now, take this, we are nearly home, my friend."

With Ivan's persuasion, Ciabhan slumped back, pale but quiet at last.

Waiting while the opiate took effect, Ivan finally stood when convinced his friend was calm. He wiped his eyes on the hem of his cloak. God, he needed to bathe! He could smell his own stink. The conditions in the shelter disgusted him. If they left their personal hygiene much longer they would all be dead, not just Ciabhan. He barked an order:

"You two, over here. Get My Lord out onto the deck in the fresh air. If he's much longer in there, he won't make the next ten minutes let alone land!" He whirled on them, his fury taking them by surprise. "God's blood! will you move?"

Ivan rarely raised his voice. By nature a patient and controlled man, he was a force to be reckoned with when angered, as his few enemies had found to their cost. A man who preferred the moderate approach to conflict was a rarity indeed in medieval England.

To the Turkish retainers he said, "Quick, get him cleaned and bring fresh bedding." As an afterthought he added, "If there is any!"

Extremely loyal to Ciabhan, he knew he was safe in their hands. Meanwhile he took the distraught Alain aside, telling him gravely, "Ciabhan is critical; his life lies in the balance. The wounds must be cleansed and dressed. He can be saved but time is running out, my friend! Listen carefully and do just as I say. Our journey is nearly done and we must move fast. As soon as we tie up, get ready four of the strongest to ride ahead with you to Compton Berry. A chamber is to be made ready with plentiful hot water and fresh linen. Kick the lazy dogs that run the place into order! Time is our enemy!" Alain nodded as Ivan continued: "It's imperative that all is ready by the time I arrive with Ciabhan. Take all the horses you need, and carts." Tossing him a bag of coins Ivan added: "Take only the best!"

Within the hour they had made land. Pacing the small landing stage, Ivan looked around him. Weary, grubby men unloaded supplies while the small tavern did a roaring trade, the serving wenches giggling at the attention.

Ivan allowed himself the luxury of a wry smile. Surveying the busy scene he was relieved that the journey appeared not to have dampened the men's ardour or their capacity for wit.

Glad to be on terra firma once more, the fleeting thought of a hot tub crossed Ivan's mind. He had endured some appalling conditions at times – extreme heat, thirst and hunger – but surely being wet through for weeks on end must count among the worst. His feet felt like lead and the damp leather of his boots cut into the blisters that the constant wet had aggravated. The clothes on his back were encrusted with salt and his eyes watered constantly from the incessant wind.

A commotion caught his attention. Cursing, he pulled his cloak tight and hurried to where Ciabhan lay. Once more Ivan tried to comfort his friend: "My Lord, you must be still. If your wounds open more, God and all his saints in heaven won't be able to save you."

Even with the drug in his bloodstream Ciabhan's strength was exceptional and he pulled Ivan to him. "Leave me!" he rasped into Ivan's ear, "for I am done!"

Ivan, desperate to keep his friend alive, clutched at his shoulders and whispered, "Not yet, My Lord. Did you not promise me good hunting in your woods?"

Struggling to breathe, Ciabhan continued, his words coming slowly and deliberately, "I have no fear of death, Brother. I am content to die now here on England's soil – the soil upon which walks my lady. Shrive me now or leave! I prepare to meet my maker!" Ciabhan collapsed back exhaling noisily as he did so.

It took a few moments for Ivan to absorb his words. As the significance of the words became clear, Ivan was mortified. He fumbled with the strings on the pouch of drugs before giving more to the semi-conscious Ciabhan.

Staggering to his feet, Ivan irritably shouted a command to those caring for the stricken man: "All is ready for My Lord to travel. Watch him constantly. He must survive, and I hold you all responsible!"

Unused to the harsh tone of this competent man, the group stopped what they were doing and watched as he walked to his horse, seemingly detached from the whole scene. Before mounting and with rising frustration he had looked towards the heavens, as if for divine guidance. A weak glimmer of light shone from a lone ray of watery sunshine, while the evening's clouds gathered for the coming dusk.

Ivan's dark features darkened even more as blood rushed to the surface of his skin, and his black eyes flashed. "A woman!" he murmured to himself. "God's blood, a woman!" So this whole nightmare had been for a woman! Ivan bit his lip to stop from blaspheming out loud, nearly drawing blood. "Why?" he asked himself. "Why had Ciabhan not stayed in the warmth of Sicily and made the journey when well? Then he could have returned in triumph – not like this, a pitiful shadow of his former self, stretchered home to die in a rundown manor while the object of his desire was blissfully unaware of his torment. Sir Ciabhan was, after all, still a Knight Templar and women were forbidden him. Obviously his love for the Lady Faye was stronger than Ivan had realised, so this was not just a game of courtly romance; they were on very dangerous ground indeed. Ivan hoisted himself into the saddle muttering to himself, "He will not die! I, Ivan dei Romani Scuri will not let him die!" Ivan determined to do all in his power to keep his friend alive, and if that meant involving the Lady Faye then so be it!

With a backward glance to check on Ciabhan and the escort, he spurred his mount in the direction of Compton Berry. Impatiently he wiped away the tears that flowed from his eyes and ran freely down his cheeks as he rode, still believing them to be suffering from the salt borne on the sea wind.

The castle of Compton Berry loomed out of the darkness as the horsemen rounded the last turn at the bottom of the steep path. Lights shone across the grassy swathe from the arched gateway and servants waited to aid their master – exactly as Ivan had commanded. Alain had done his job well. The young knight helped carry the ailing Ciabhan into the castle's sanctuary.

"As quick as you can, Alain," said Ivan. "There is much to do!"

During the last hour's ride, Ivan had made a decision.

When Ciabhan had been stretchered into a warm chamber, he took Alain aside and said urgently, "A message must be got to the Lady Faye at Pagons Ton. Pray God she is there! He has called her name constantly in his delirium. Will you help me, Alain?"

Alain replied, "Whatever it takes, sir. I'd ride through hell itself if it would save him!"

Within the hour Alain was riding hard for Pagons Ton, the bearer of a letter. Innocent in its information, the message stated clearly how her champion, Sir Ciabhan of Compton Berry, now lay near death, and that his final wish was that she inherit all his earthly chattels. It was felt by those caring for him that it was therefore right that the Lady Faye and her husband, Leon, be made aware of his imminent demise, as they might wish to make an effort to see him, assuming it was not already too late. Ivan had signed the letter using the name she would remember him by: Brother Ivan dei Romani Scuri.

What Ivan, in all his wisdom, had not reckoned for was the determination and willpower of the lovely woman he had met in the garden of the convent those long months ago.

She arrived before daybreak, having ridden through the darkness with Alain, a local guide and one of the Turks. Distraught at the news, her face had been pale in the moonlight as she had asked, "Ivan, tell me please, my sweet lord lives – that I am not too late!"

Ivan led her to where Ciabhan lay unconscious. Shocked at his condition, her hands flew to her face.

Moments later she threw off her travelling cloak, rolled up her sleeves and said, "Come, Brother, we have a precious life to save this day."

Shadowy figures came and went as quietly as shadows in the confines of the sickroom, bringing hot water, clean dressings, and astringents. Beside the man who lay so desperately ill in the centre of the room, Faye and Ivan began the fight to save his life.

Ciabhan had already been cleaned, his wounds dressed

and his comfort administered to. No one had been confident enough to remove the belt from Ciabhan's waist, beneath which lay the deepest wound. Even Ivan was reluctant, for fear of the bleeding that would follow.

Seeing his apprehension, Faye spoke firmly: "Make sure your blade is sharp and your hand steady, sir, for, like it or not, this must come off!" She smiled reassuringly.

Even with a warning, Ivan had been unprepared for the bleeding that followed. Of course, he had seen blood loss in bucketfuls on the battlefield, but nothing had prepared him for this horror. For the rest of his life he would be haunted by the sight and smell of that sickroom, as Ciabhan's lifeblood splashed away. As fast as dressings were applied they became saturated with the blood, so red. It darkened wad after wad of white linen with its sticky sweetness. All their expertise was needed to staunch the flood.

The day was well advanced as the flow gradually ran to a trickle, and the room was quiet as Ivan had stole a look at Faye. Her hair, blood-matted, stuck to her cheeks where she had drawn despairing hands across her face; and now, weary from the endless hours, she rested her head on the edge of the bed.

Softly, across his friend's sleeping body, Ivan spoke gently: "Faye, you are exhausted. He sleeps now. There is nothing more to do. He is in God's hands."

Faye looked up with hollow circled eyes. Weakly she shook her head as she tried to stand. "No, Brother, I'll not leave his side until I am sure he lives." Tenderly she bent and kissed Ciabhan's forehead, touching his cheek as she whispered, pleadingly, "Stay with us, my sweet lord. We are nothing without you." Then she knelt once more amongst the tatters of blood-soaked belt on the floor. With hands clasped, she remained so until dusk, watching as the gold crucifix at Ciabhan's neck rose and fell with each breath he struggled to take.

Winter slowly gave way to warmer days, and Mother Nature blessed the valley around Compton Berry with welcome warmth, bringing vigour to the slowly recovering

Ciabhan. Mother Nature could not, of course, take all the credit for this; Ciabhan's recovery had undoubtedly been hastened by the presence of Faye.

Pleased that his decision had been the right one, Ivan could now leave his friend's side confident that Faye would take care of his every need. He rejoiced to see Ciabhan smile in the company of this woman, and once again the two men enjoyed each other's company over wine in the evenings.

On one particularly mild morning, Faye had said, "I think it would benefit My Lord to be outside today. The chamber can be cleaned. He will do well to take some air."

Carried into a sheltered and secluded area, the sun soon chased away Ciabhan's pallor, bringing colour to cheeks starved of sun. At his side, Faye chatted and read. Entertaining him with her wit, she brought amusement to the convalescing knight. If they discussed their growing fondness for each other, Ivan did not know, but it was apparent for all to see – as clear as the sweet-smelling yellow roses that rambled over the mossy wall, filling the garden with the fragrance of love. Proud of his part in reuniting once more Faye and Ciabhan, Ivan watched them together. Harmony seemed at last to reign over the three of them, and his own contentment was complete. To the woman cleaning the room he said, without turning, "They make a handsome pair, think you not?"

Mati stopped her toil and joined Ivan, looking on the couple as they conversed. The sun shone on the man's chestnut hair as he inclined his head to that of the woman, who in turn lifted her face adoringly. Carefully Mati answered the man she had first met at the convent of the Sisters of Poverty: "Love, sir, is in the hands of God. We mortals rarely choose where our hearts lie. When we do, we make mistakes!" She looked woefully in the direction of her husband, Torr, scattering rushes on the swept floor. He glowered back at her, jealousy obvious as she spoke with the fine-looking knight. Ivan smiled kindly as she sighed with resignation and went back to her duties.

Green spring drifted into humid summer, and August's fair weather made for a bountiful harvest. Endless summer days passed in a haze of gold, nourishing the mind and body alike.

They settled into the routine of manor life, and one of their first chores was to make good the little chapel, neglected for so long. Taking charge, Ivan succeeded in restoring its inner peace, making it once more a place of spirituality. Rededicated for the act of worship, the first service was in thanks for Ciabhan's life – a joyful service, which the whole household attended. The chapel, with its marble altar draped in simple linen, became Ivan's domain, and his priority. It was a place of sanctuary and contemplation. A symbolic sign for both men was Ciabhan's shield, which hung on the wall, its Christian cross blood-red upon the white.

Ciabhan had given Faye a choice of room, and she had chosen a light, airy solar at the top of a steep flight of stairs. The oak door opened onto the high roof overlooking the valley to the west, where she could gaze across the hills; or to the east, where lapped the sea.

The whole castle benefited from a woman's touch, and the previously tired little castle, in its veil of green forest, shone with freshness. Ciabhan's personal standard snapped proudly on the highest point.

Fed and cared for, the villagers under obligation to the manor worked hard for their master, glad to have order and discipline back at last. Long missing in the valley, the sound of the lute could be heard on lazy evenings. To most it was obvious that the Lady Faye had fallen under the spell of Compton Berry, as well as under that of its master.

Letters written to her husband had been ignored, and Leon's last words to her as she'd ridden away with Alain haunted her still: "Go now, Faye, and you will never return, ever! I will not be dishonoured by your tainted reputation!"

The hatred her husband felt for Ciabhan, his former friend, was groundless and inexcusable. Her patience exhausted, no longer able to defend or forgive his behaviour, she stopped writing. Choosing to stay at Compton Berry, she at last embraced her true feelings for Sir Ciabhan. By his own irrational actions, Leon had effectively driven his wife into the waiting arms of his perceived enemy, the Templar.

Sharp showers during the night had left the delicate leaves on the tall beeches hanging like little lanterns. In shades of green they shivered and shook on the spidery saplings as the wind soughed high in the treetops.

On a horse for the first time since his illness, Ciabhan had led Faye's little mare deeper into the woods than she had ever been. The undergrowth had pulled at her skirts, scratching her unprotected legs. As the faint sound of thunder rumbled through the humid air she spoke: "My Lord, it's a little overgrown here and I fear rain is on the way. It would do you no good to be caught in a deluge."

Without stopping, his voice carried back to her: "Madam, you nag too much! Am I to live the life of a decrepit, to wither and waste away through lack of action?"

She sighed with exasperation, "Men!"

A few paces more and Ciabhan halted, turned to meet her gaze and opened his mouth to speak again. At that moment a fat raindrop plopped onto his head, ran down his nose and disappeared into his beard. She smiled behind her hand as he reached for her reins. Shaking the rain from his nose, he grinned broadly. "It seems that you are right again, My Lady!" His hand brushed hers as he led the horses out of the tangle into the clearing.

A run-down hunter's lodge nestled forlornly under a dripping, moss-covered thatch. Faye looked around her as the rain began in earnest. Heavy raindrops sat like jewels on the myriad leaves, hanging for seconds before sliding off to disappear into the ever thirsty forest floor. With girlish enthusiasm she slipped from the saddle into the knee-high woodland grass, and, as the rain ran down her hair and face, she gazed upwards at the vaulting green. "This is a cathedral, Ciabhan, a dazzling natural cathedral. Surely God's own hand has touched this place with perfection."

As he had hoped, her reaction had been one of wonderment. Smiling his rare smile, he said tenderly, "I waited to share its beauty with you, Faye, until now, for I knew that you would love it, and I wanted to enjoy your reaction."

Her delight was palpable and Ciabhan watched as the warm rain cascaded over her body, causing the thin summer clothes to cling to her. Like a faery creature she swayed and twirled. Desire overtook him and stirred his loins without warning. Suddenly he wanted to hold her more than anything, to feel her body in his arms. His breathing came in short gasps, as an ecstatic Faye held out her arms to him. Yellow flashes lit the dark backdrop of the forest clearing, long before the thunder announced its arrival.

Squelching to the lodge, Ciabhan circled Faye's waist protectively with his arm as he guided her, bedraggled and shivering, to cover. Unable to contain his mirth longer he had laughed, "My dear, you look a very sorry sight indeed – enough to frighten Lucifer himself!"

She found it hard to control her pleasure as he wiped the rain carefully from her face, his own still dripping with water. Taking off his cloak, Faye trembled at his touch, as he draped it around her shoulders. Fixing him with her sternest stare, she'd mockingly scolded, "And you, sir, are no Saint Michael!"

As they laughed, their eyes locked and he bent to kiss her, but before their lips had touched the silence was broken by a barn owl that flew low over their heads. Disturbed from her roost, her great eyes looked down haughtily as she headed to the misty beeches. Faye had stumbled in shock but Ciabhan was instantly alert. Dagger in hand, he had prepared to defend her, shielding her body with his. Lifting her to her feet he did not let her go immediately. She felt an urgency in his touch as if he wished to say something but had decided against it.

Alarmed, she looked around. "Is something wrong, sir?" she said.

Ciabhan replied, still holding her tightly, "No, nothing

to fear. Are you hurt?"

She assured him all was well, her hazel eyes shining with the colours of the forest as it wrapped around the two of them. "Dear Ciabhan, in truth I have never felt happier."

She would remember for ever the moment he placed his lips on her own hungry mouth. Savouring every caress, her body yielded eagerly to his as the rain washed over them in silver sheets. Wispy threads of vapour curled eerily between the trees like spectres, as water-laden leaves dribbled their rivers into the sodden earth. The steady drip was joined by birdsong, faintly at first, until it filled the glade, joyful at the passing of the squall. Countless hours of separation and unrequited longing had prepared each for this moment, and now, truly alone for the first time, the words tumbled from their lips; declarations of love were accompanied by kisses. No longer having to rely on furtive glances and touches, they embraced, caressing each other with sheer and utter delight.

Hands tightly clasped, they emerged from the dank lodge into the spectacular setting, and, in that blissful place, the silent trees his witness, Ciabhan knelt at Faye's feet and pledged his troth in a scene reminiscent of the romance of King Arthur. "In truth and honour, I worship at your feet, Faye, and shall not rest until you are my wife."

She joined him on her knees and together they faced each other, the sun dancing upon the Templar cross that Ciabhan took from around his neck and placed around that of Faye. Nestling between her breasts, it lay polished and shiny on the azure of her gown as she replied, "I think you jest, my dear! Forget not that I am already wedded. Indeed, to be your wife would make me the happiest woman in Christendom, but free I am not!"

He led her towards the tethered horses, and smiled as he held the stirrup for her. Once mounted she looked down. Little bits of moss hung in his hair and his cloak was grubby where it had doubled as a cover for her to sit on. His eyes were large and bright and, when looked at deeply, almost too beautiful for a man – especially a man of war!

"You will be my wife with every afforded honour, Faye. Be assured, we will be wed – this I pledge."

She silently prayed to Mother Mary for willpower, knowing that for this man she would have willingly forgone her honour.

The community at Compton Berry was a thriving hive of industry. Men gathered as nature's bounty ripened, and by the misty dawn of Michaelmas the harvest was nearly complete.

Autumn bought many pleasures, and for Faye one of these was the collecting of mushrooms from dewy fields. On misty mornings Faye and Mati would set out early, returning with full baskets of the fungi with their pungent musty aroma as the sun burnt off the morning's chill fog. In the afternoon they scrambled amongst hedges that had caught the hot morning sun and plucked juicy blackberries from vicious thorny brambles.

Faye recalled her mother telling her, "You can only pick in September, never in October, for the Devil pees on them then." Faye liked to believe that myth, and would not dream of gathering then! She smiled at the foolishness of the saying.

Red-breasted robins, winter's bright heralds, flashed through the berry-laden hedges, their song a reminder of shortening days. Black, seedy splodges, deposited by birds, dotted the paths and walls, and the sweet smell of preserve permeated the castle kitchen as apple and blackberry combined in every way possible.

Side by side on a mellow autumnal day, Ciabhan and Faye neared the castle after a morning spent visiting the resident priest at the Church of Saint Mary in Totnes. A moderate man, he was sympathetic to Ciabhan's issues and they had become firm allies.

Faye dreamily absorbed the sights, happy in the company of the man she loved. Beneath tall chestnut trees, those sentinels of the landscape, they walked the horses at a leisurely pace home to Compton Berry. Faye marvelled at the majesty of the imposing trees and made a mental note of the impending crop, looking up at the fat spiky cases ripening on the drooping branches.

Ciabhan, attuned to Faye's humours, knew instinctively that she was a happy woman on this lovely day. Loath to spoil it, he hesitated over what he had to say. She would be upset, of that he was positive. So, sure of her reaction, he had left telling her of his intentions until now. Slowing his mount, he turned to face her. "Faye, in two days' time I leave for Rome!" He held his breath.

"We leave for where?" she said, puzzled. "Where did you say?"

Quickly he repeated himself. "You misheard me, Faye. I leave for Rome in two days, alone! My mind is made up. It will not be changed!"

One look at his face, his mouth set in a hard and stubborn line, told her that she had not misheard. She opened her mouth to speak but no words came. The day was in a moment ruined, on the whim of a man. She knew better than to argue. Tears stung her eyes and she was weeping still as they rode silently beneath the gate.

Ivan, from the chapel window, could tell that Ciabhan had broken the news, but he decided that discretion was the better part of valour and kept out of the way. Angry that Ciabhan had wished to make such a journey so soon, Ivan had begged to be taken with him; but Ciabhan, adamant that he was the only man he could entrust Faye to, would have none of it. He must stay behind and care for Faye. Nursemaid to a woman! It was not a duty he relished.

To Faye, Ciabhan had tried to explain: "Faye, I want us to be married in the eyes of God, and you afforded the honour you deserve." Still new to Ciabhan, the words of love came with difficulty and he struggled to explain to the tearful Faye. Intense, he lifted her from her horse and took her in his arms, trying to calm her with kind words: "More than anything, I want you for my wife, but this can only be done with the dissolution of your loveless marriage to Leon, and the severing of my Templar vows. This is the fresh beginning we both want."

Trying to understand his reasoning, she stammered between her sobs, "You know that I care nothing for my reputation. I would be happy to live with you out of wedlock. I beg you, Ciabhan, take me with you. I can look after you," she pleaded, using all of her feminine wiles. But to no avail – Ciabhan's mind was made up. Committed to the journey to Rome, he listened to her reasoning as she whispered her concerns: "Rome is so distant and, though you are recovered, you are far from the peak of fitness. Think on it afresh, I beg you, Ciabhan. I could not bear to lose you again." Even her tears falling hot onto his skin would not shake his resolve, and Faye's pleading was in vain. It was his testimony of love, and this his way of proving it. He sat dejected as she attacked his plan. "I am no simpering maiden that you must prove yourself to! That you are here against the odds is proof enough! Please, Ciabhan, let us be together in love. What care I for reputation?" Taking his hands in hers she knelt at his feet. "Take me," she beseeched.

Lifting her hands, he kissed the fingers, and replied, "No! Never would I risk your safety. I ask only that your prayers go with me."

Seeing the battle lost, she took the emerald ring that she had worn constantly since he had placed it on her finger, and answered softly, "That you should even ask, My Lord, does me an injustice!"

She held out the brilliant jewel to its rightful owner, but he would not take it. "The ring is yours, Faye," he objected.

But she persisted: "The first time I ever saw you, this ring was on your finger. Its comfort carried me through lonely days, for in its radiance lived your image and the hope that we would meet again. Now I carry you in my heart. Take it, Ciabhan, and I shall dwell in its depths until you return."

Reluctantly he took the ring, and once again the emerald sat on Ciabhan's finger; the dramatic green square glinted with all the hues of forest and sea.

Hours before he left, they spent some time talking and planning for a future that for Faye seemed an eternity away. Studying the emerald, Ciabhan asked, "Promise you will not weep for me, Faye. It's your strength and thoughts of our marriage that will sustain me in trouble, and I need look no further than here for your image." Holding her in his strong embrace, they stood as one. "Now let me go, woman, for I swear a moment longer and God himself couldn't tear me from your arms. I leave before sunrise."

True to his word, Ciabhan had long gone by the time a watery sun broke over the topmost branches of the larch wood, which now looked a little sparse as thin brittle twigs were shaken free of their tenacious hold. They fell to the forest floor, joining the small pine cones already there.

The void left by Ciabhan's departure to some degree was filled by Ivan, who, also resentful of being left behind, had joined her in self-pity.

During one conversation she had remonstrated with him: "I can't believe, Ivan, that you agreed to let him travel so far so soon!"

Coldly he had responded, "And do you think I didn't plead to be taken!" His black eyes flashed. "Do you really think, madam, that I wanted to stay behind as a nursemaid?" Regretting the words instantly as he saw the hurt in her eyes, he turned away.

Careless words spoken in anger should not be allowed to foster ill feeling. With her most disarming smile, Faye touched gently the sleeve of Ivan's tunic and said to the brooding figure, "Well, my dear Ivan, it seems you and I must make the best of this situation, like it or not!"

He scowled, his tension obvious.

Undeterred, she took his arm confidently. "Come, Brother, let us walk together a while."

Easily she chatted by his side, and as they left the cool of the great hall she felt his resistance weakening. When serious, Ivan's face became hard. The normally mobile features took on the appearance of a sculpture, beautiful and unworldly, and as cold as marble.

The castle was alive with everyday life and cheery hellos had to be acknowledged. By the time they reached the postern in the west-facing wall Ivan's mood had lightened.

Beyond the postern door, the ground dropped away. It was dangerous in places, but for the sure-footed it presented few challenges. Ivan looked down. A pond glittered far below. Beginning the descent, his feet slipped as he plunged close on the heels of Faye, convinced now that she was a woman possessed!

"God's blood, Faye, I'm to guard your life, not end it!"

Ragged and scratched, Ivan came to a halt at the stream's edge as it ran between the slope and the village pond.

"Ciabhan would have my guts," he gasped with a backward look up the dangerous slope. With one arm locked around the low branch of a tree, he examined his sandal-shod feet. From beneath his fringe he saw her smile. "Jest not, My Lady! Any harm that comes to you I pay for – no doubt with my life!"

Wickedly she tried pulling him from his tenuous hold. "Come, Brother, you fuss like an old woman! And besides, Ciabhan loves you as much as he does me!"

Suddenly Ivan threw back his head and roared with laughter. White teeth flashed in his brown face as the lively Ivan returned.

Once over the stream, they sat on the bank of the pond. Faye trailed her fingers in the cooling water while Ivan rolled onto his back, folding his arms beneath his head. The willows hid them from view, but the voices of children carried across the pond as they played at its edges. For a while Ivan was transported back to his childhood as the white clouds scudded across the pale-blue ether.

Faye noticed how scarred his forearms were, and she imagined him and Ciabhan fighting together. The thought made her shudder.

Still gazing at the sky, Ivan spoke, his voice low. "When Ciabhan was so ill, he promised me that we would hunt in the woods of Compton Berry. I must hold him to that pledge!"

A kingfisher flashed across the green waters, its jewel colours reminding her of the emerald, and of Ciabhan. She would pray and light a candle for him tonight in the little chapel. An idea came to her and she shared it with Ivan: "I will document our story, Ivan – all that has happened to us. It will help me bear his absence. The belt will be my inspiration. What say you, Ivan? Is this not a good idea?" She sought his approval, continuing: "The manuscript will be my gift to Ciabhan on the day of our wedding, concluding our story, for the belt told only half."

The autumn air warmed unseasonably, and sun filtered through long ribbons of willow, and fell like dancing diamonds on the water. Ivan turned and smiled indulgently, deep in his own thoughts.

The Raven had become the name used by the household to describe Ivan. His black hair and penchant for black garb was the obvious connection, but he also possessed an uncanny knack of being everywhere at once – or so it seemed to simple folk! Not all were aware that Brother Ivan was, first and foremost, a committed man of God – a monk. He had travelled to England, his sole aim being to become a Knight Templar, having already taken vows. Ivan had connections with many influential members of the Church in Rome, and it was to these that Ciabhan now went carrying papers containing valid reasons for an annulment of Faye's marriage.

"These will get you introductions to the right people, my friend, and I see no barriers to an annulment being granted," Ivan had reassured Ciabhan. At Ivan's request, Ciabhan also carried long-overdue letters to his parents.

In the absence of Ciabhan, Ivan proved a fair custodian of Compton Berry. Treading a complex path between acting master and spiritual mentor, he kept harmony within the household. Diffusing petty squabbles was easy, and Faye's diplomacy proved a great help to him in many cases. Keeping Ciabhan's now thriving estate safe from opportunists was more difficult, and he regularly patrolled its boundaries with a group of men he had armed. Five

Sicilian seamen had stayed behind at Compton Berry.

Faye spent long winter days writing in her solar, from time to time coming down to the great hall to sit by the warmth of the spitting fire. Wrapped in fur, she would read her day's work to Ivan, and he would listen intently as great flames danced. Mulled wine warming chilled hands, they would converse in the glow of the fire, until inevitably their thoughts turned to Ciabhan. The evening meal was prepared around them with a cheerful clatter.

Casting his eyes across the hall, Ivan said one evening, "Mati's husband seems a disagreeable fellow. He avoids me when he can, and only ever grunts!"

Faye followed Ivan's eyes to the man dragging in another great bundle of wood. "It's me he blames for causing Mati's flight from the house in Pagons Ton. He was devoted to Leon, and is still his man. I fear poor Mati's life is not a happy one. That's why I keep her close."

"Mati appears to be no fool, Faye. Why did she not leave him in Pagons Ton or send him to warn Leon?" Ivan queried.

Faye answered immediately: "Fear, I suppose – after all, Leon had threatened to hang him if harm came to me, and Ciabhan had threatened to cut his throat. Both men would have carried out their threats without hesitation! Who would have guessed it was Halbert who posed the threat?"

Ivan thought a while, his fingertips together on his lips, before replying, "Ciabhan, obviously!" he said.

On the rare occasions that the weather allowed during the winter, Ivan and Faye rode into Totnes. They walked on the jetty where Ciabhan had lain so ill on his return from Sicily. In the small tavern on the quayside, Ivan bought refreshment and introduced her to seamen who had endured the journey with them. Hungry for news of Ciabhan, she devoured the tales Ivan related of the travels and skirmishes they had shared, but always she remained sad that he was so distant from her side.

At times she joined Ivan in discussion with brothers from the great abbey which lay to the west, a few miles from Totnes. Ivan's intellect was formidable, and she listened in awe to his theological reasoning. It was hardly surprising that Ciabhan had found his company so enjoyable; they had much in common.

On the way home, when he seemed lost in thought, she would seek to cheer him, and she would tease: "Come, Brother, teach me how to think and reason like a man, that I may better understand the mystifying ways of the Almighty."

He would look at her and shake his head in mock frustration. "I fear that you, My Lady, would give even God a run for his money!"

Faye and Mati would occasionally take the road into the town and scour the stalls at the market held across from the guildhall, as they used to do in Pagons Ton. Amongst the trinkets and baubles Faye would try to uncover something of interest for Ivan, as a way of thanking him for his patience with her. On one of these trips she found an oval stone cloak clasp, of the truest blue with flecks of gold running through it.

So thrilled was Ivan, that he fastened it immediately to his cloak, scolding her for wasting money on him. By the festival of Christmas, only one letter had made its way to Compton Berry from Ciabhan. Its contents gave enormous comfort to Faye, and she read it again and again. It warmed her as the castle froze. She wondered if her letter had been received. He had made no mention of them!

Gradually Faye's manuscript took shape. On the whole she enjoyed reliving the past. Some memories unfortunately were not pleasant, but they had to be written if it was to be a truthful account. She declared to Mati, "This really is a labour of love, Mati. I do believe the effort is greater than that which went into the belt's embroidery!"

When not at her escritoire, Faye could be found busying herself around the castle. Having found her forte in caring for the sick and weak, she made sure that the healing plants were tended and in constant supply, even organising a small infirmary in some quiet unused rooms, where the sick could be ministered to.

Ivan showed his approval and helped willingly, glad that her energy was being used to good effect.

Faye never again ventured into the special place deep in the woods; it remained for her and Ciabhan alone. When she yearned for its solitude, she would instead make the descent down the slope to sit or walk beneath the willows by the pond.

Ivan always knew where to find her.

As the month of May approached, Ivan remembered Ciabhan's request: "If I am not back by May, make plans for My Lady's birthday. I fear she will not wish for celebrations, but ignore that! The days will be lengthening and the time will be right for merrymaking with or without me!"

Ivan promised he would not forget.

Ciabhan must have foreseen Faye's depression, for as the month she loved approached, a cloud settled over her. Not even the returning swifts and swallows, or the call of the cuckoo as she haunted the reed beds could lift her darkening spirits. Instead of joy at nature's rebirth, she constantly sought reassurance that Ciabhan was returning. Questioning Ivan, she would demand, "Tell me truly, sir, is there something you are withholding from me?"

Filling the air with their sweet delicious aroma, lambs were spit-roasted on the open green in front of the castle. Impatient red-faced boys sat rotating the hot iron spit, watching enviously as their friends played, awaiting their turn.

From the castle walls bunting fluttered in the cool breeze, while above them Ciabhan's standard flew, its bright silk a constant reminder of their still absent master.

In the middle of the green the maypole stood proudly. Garlands of country flowers and foliage curled around the pole, and from the gold crown at the top dangled the long coloured ribbons. They attracted the attention of pretty young girls in their best dresses, who couldn't resist the pretty colours and waited their turn to dance, giggling in eager little groups.

"I'm glad to see some colour in your cheeks at last, My Lady," said Ivan cheerfully to Faye as they strolled amongst the revelry.

"The air is warm," she had said. "There is delight in such gaiety, but think not that I am happy!"

Her reply had been typical of her mood lately. Ivan looked pensive; if this jollity failed to lift her gloom, then the chances of her enjoying her forthcoming birthday seemed remote. He wished Ciabhan were here. He struggled to constantly reassure – and, besides, he was getting a little apprehensive himself for Ciabhan's safety. Why hadn't his friend taken him? Alain and one of the Turks would have been enough to protect Faye!

He took her arm and turned her to face him. "You are not the only one who misses Ciabhan, Faye! Be strong. He will return. Remember he has a marriage to plan for!"

Guilty and ashamed at her self-pity, she apologised for being such miserable company. "Forgive me, Ivan. I forget this pain is not mine only. I have been very selfish!"

He smiled his brilliant smile. They walked on together. Music from the minstrel group gradually lightened their mood.

Watching the proceedings from the walkway that stretched the length of the curtain wall, Torr turned to his wife and scowled: "I see it hasn't taken your fine lady long to find another heart to break!"

A special effort had gone into the preparations for Faye's birthday, and a banquet with dancing had been secretly planned for the evening.

Bunting from May Day still festooned the castle grounds so nothing seemed unusual, and the secret was safe as Faye and Ivan rode out on her special day. As the month progressed she had tried to lift her spirits, if only for the sake of Ivan, who had been so understanding towards her. With demons of his own to fight, he remained at all times courteous and tolerant to the woman in his care.

She slept badly, keeping her fears for Ciabhan's safety to herself, praying in silence night after night.

Following the river that rushed and twinkled beside them, they enjoyed a leisurely ride to the great Abbey of Buckfast. Free of the confines of the castle, Faye enjoyed her day out. Ivan was good company and on this, her special day, she was in very good humour. Drawing close to the abbey, she marvelled at its towering magnificence. Casting her eyes upwards, she felt dwarfed and humbled by its sheer size. Tightly she held on to the reins as the spires giddily raced across the sky. Against the wooded backdrop, the beautiful abbey sat amidst the fresh green of May, shining in the bright sunshine.

It had not escaped Ivan's notice how much the abbey had impressed her. "Careful, My Lady, it would be far from graceful if you were to fall from the saddle! And as you are still in my care it could prove dangerous – for me!" He laughed as he held his arm protectively at her back.

"Danger has given me a wide berth in your care, dear Ivan," she smiled, taking his hand as they rode under the dazzling stained-glass windows.

In the gardens, Faye met Friar Jaime, a Spaniard, who spent his days tending the rare medicinal plants brought and cultivated from his native land. Later he took her to see the winemakers, where she watched with fascination the process that produced the famous Buckfast wine. "Madam, you will do me the honour of taking some with you?" he said.

Ivan watched as Faye charmed the brothers, glad that she at last was smiling. "It would seem that half the year's produce was given to you, Faye," observed Ivan, gesturing to the heavily laden cart rattling along behind them. "Wine, honey, herbs, salves – the list goes on, madam!" His eyes twinkled. He suggested that she had bewitched the brothers.

Her skin glowed in the first sun of summer. Happily she turned to him. "No witchery, sir! They were exceedingly generous, insisting that I take all they offered. One even gave me fresh parchment on learning of my writing."

Little gold wires danced in her ears and beads of amber sparkled at their ends, complementing the deep yellow of her cape and the sun's blush on her cheek. Bobbing against her head, the hood had gradually worked loose, revealing her hair, and it was strange how today he had noticed the two golden combs that held those locks from her face. The sun glinted on flecks of red and gold amongst the dark brown. How attractive Faye was! Ciabhan really was a very lucky man.

"Today has been a delight. Thank you for making it so, Ivan."

"I have enjoyed it too, but it is Ciabhan who should be thanked. He left explicit instructions for your birthday to be a day of pleasure if he were not here to share it with you. As usual, he thought of everything, Faye."

She looked straight ahead, but he could see that her eyes were bursting with tears. They filled her eyes and threatened to spill down her cheeks, but bravely she kept them in check, saying, "Without you, then, Brother, I should have had a truly miserable day!"

Music spilled out of gates and over walls as the sound of merrymaking filled the valley. Those not inside danced or relaxed on the green, enjoying the hospitality provided in celebration of Faye's birthday. Her joy had been evident from the moment she and Ivan had started down the long path.

Seeing Mati and the household gathered, she dismounted and greeted them all with kisses. Ivan sat and watched as she was swept along by excitable females. He struggled to keep her yellow dress in sight. Today had been a great success, but Ciabhan should have been here enjoying her embrace of thanks.

Privately Ivan was becoming a little concerned for his friend. Leon and his henchmen approached the castle cautiously. Never having met Ivan, Leon was nonetheless familiar with the renown of the Raven, and was not about to underestimate his adversary.

The watch at the castle entrance had been easily

overpowered; the horses' muffled hooves deadened any sound. With no time to raise the alarm, the attack had been swift and brutal, and the guards were clubbed to the ground.

Leon and his group rode under the gatehouse and into the bailey casually, as if they were late arrivals. Unchallenged, Leon stood at the entrance to the hall and watched as Faye moved gracefully in the middle of a group of dancers.

Starting forward with an air of confidence, he mused, 'This is going to be easier than I thought!'

Leon heard nothing as the Raven stepped from the shadows. He felt only the point of a sword pressing into his back as Ivan spoke: "And what brings you, sir, so late and uninvited to the home of Sir Ciabhan of Compton Berry? Think you that we would be unprepared?"

"My wife! I have come for my wife!" replied Leon coolly.

"As you wish!" said Ivan. "The lady is free to go where she pleases. Ask her yourself."

Faye, surprised, had seen the drama unfold and she hurried over. "My Lord, what brings you here so tardy?"

The music had stopped and the room, so lively a moment ago, was now hushed as all faces turned to the doorway. Faye looked upon her husband for the first time in nearly a year.

Leon complained: "Perhaps you could prevail on your manservant to remove the point of his sword from my back, madam. I am unarmed."

The insult to Ivan's status was deliberate and Faye saw him bristle.

Leon continued contemptuously: "These foreigners often possess souls as dark as their faces. It is strange that the great Sir Ciabhan should find their company so agreeable, think you not, madam?"

Faye's reply was curt. "I think, sir, that insults do not become you. Come now, take my arm that we may talk. Presumably you are here to offer me birthday greetings!"

With a scything look at Ivan, Leon brushed himself down

and, with a smug smile curling his lips, let Faye lead him across the hall and outside into the kitchen garden.

"Why now, Leon? Why now?" Faye demanded of him when settled. She watched her husband intently; the man beside her was not the husband she had once been so proud of. She pulled away as he tried to take her hand, wondering what had ever made her young heart do somersaults in her chest. His eyes, once the colour of summer skies, now looked cold and devoid of feeling as they darted from side to side with an edginess bordering on the paranoid, unable to look into her own. And his swarthy features, in youth so open and appealing, were now decidedly sour. She stood, the better to make her point: "There is no going back, Leon. My mind is made up. I stay at Compton Berry; it is where I choose to be!"

The petulant tone helped his case not a jot as he spat back, "With the Templar saint and his black dog? You forget yourself, madam. You are still my wife, legally bound in the eyes of God, and I am within my rights to command your return!"

"You could try, sir!" she challenged fiercely, "but it would be to no avail!"

Ivan, from the shadows, still watched and he saw Leon nod in his direction contemptuously. "The treacherous Templar and his assassin – why steal a fellow-knight's wife? The dogs of hell have more morals!"

Finally losing her patience with his childish pique, Faye's voice was cold: "Your petty jealousy alone has ruined us, Leon. Face the truth for once – these are the men who helped when I needed it most, when my husband turned away! Be a man – accept the inevitable!"

Shamed, his tone changed. "You love him then?"

"Yes, we love each other."

Her tone was final, her eyes defiant as they flashed. He still thought her the most beautiful woman he had ever set eyes on. "Then stay where you deserve and be happy; but take heed, madam, the Templar can never love you as much as I, and be sure it will be your undoing!" Before he swaggered across the hall, he turned, and his mouth curled spitefully. "I left gifts for you – one you will love; the smaller is very personal."

Reaching Ivan, Leon demanded the return of his arms, and quietly, close to the ear of the hated Ivan, and out of hearing of all others, he hissed, "Make no mistake, you son of a devil's whore, I will have my wife! Dead or alive – it matters not to me now!"

Torr carried the box into the chamber. Without looking at Faye or his wife he placed the box at Faye's feet with a grunt, his lips curving slyly as he left the room.

"I wonder what it can be? Do open it, madam," said Mati.

Faye answered her as she unbuckled the thick leather bindings. "I think it fairly obvious, Mati. can you not hear the soft mewling?" As suspected, it contained her darling Bella Donna – the peregrine falcon she had so missed. Looking slightly the worse for wear and very sorry for herself, Bella sat hunched in the corner of the box, great eyes fearful as the light hit her.

"Oh! Faye, how thoughtful of Leon. So the man has some kindness in him after all!" exclaimed Mati, peering in at the bird. Acquainted with the falcon from old, Mati was not as enamoured as her mistress.

"You may be right," said Faye doubtfully. Her eyes had fallen on a small pouch tied to the side of the box, not immediately noticeable. This must be the small package Leon had mentioned. The last thing Faye wanted from Leon was some expensive bauble, given in the hope of luring her back. She tried removing it secretly, but Mati's keen eyes had spotted it too.

"Another gift? Methinks your husband is too eager for your return," said Mati.

Impatiently, Faye scolded her maid: "Shame on you, Mati, for even thinking I would consider it! Here!" She tossed the pouch to her maid dismissively. "You take it, for I care not to open it!"

Mati hung her head shamefully as she opened the pouch.

Faye, somewhere in the background, cooed at Bella Donna. If Mati had gasped or made some sound of surprise, Faye would have made no move to see what the pouch contained, but the dull thud on the silk carpet breaking the silence caused her to turn inquisitively. Mati, with one hand clamped over her mouth, stood, her whole body shaking as in the grip of some terrible fever, unable to utter a word.

Faye's horrified eyes followed where Mati pointed. On the floor, where it had rolled off the carpet, dazzling even against the jewel colours of the rug, lay Ciabhan's emerald ring. Sinking to her knees, Faye picked up the ring and cupped it in her hands. Closing her eyes she rocked as she held it tight to her breast. A ringing emptiness in her head filled with a sound like that of a wounded animal; like the howls of anguish heard from deep in the woods on still nights; like the moans of those led to slaughter. Only much later did she learn that the sounds were her own cries.

Slumped beside her mistress, Mati's body shook with great sobs as the misery of the situation took hold. Fearing for Faye in her desolation, Mati tried and failed to console her.

It was thus that Ivan found the two women. "In God's name, what ails you?" he asked Faye, taking her by the shoulders.

Faye looked up at the stranger before her, unable to identify the dark man. She offered no resistance as he prised open her fingers. Shaking her head, she wept over and over again, "Dead! Ciabhan's dead! My sweet lord. My sweet, sweet lord. No! No! No!"

There was no mistaking Ciabhan's emerald ring; its brilliance emphasised the paleness of the palm that held it. Anger made the blood rush to Ivan's head. He fumed and shook with barely concealed rage. Under Ivan's nose the devious Leon had taken his revenge on Faye, and Ivan had failed to protect her. Well, the gauntlet was down now! Let the fool think he had found a chink in their armour, but he would pay for this; sooner or later he would pay dearly!

Ivan questioned Faye. "Are you sure that this is Ciabhan's ring?"

But this only brought fresh lamentations. "Think you that I know not the ring I wore for so long?"

"Hush now, Faye," he replied soothingly. "Believe me, Ciabhan is not dead. I smell the devil at work."

Closing the door quietly, Mati picked up the box and carried the squawking Bella Donna outside. Replacing the felt, she set the distressed bird safely beside the parapet. She left Ivan cradling the still sobbing Faye. As his cloak spread around them, it occurred to her that he did indeed resemble a raven – the name now being used to describe him. Her mistress's sobs followed her down the stairs to her own room.

Security at Compton Berry was strengthened; Ivan immediately threw a discreet cordon around the castle, using every available man. The last thing he wanted was for Faye to feel imprisoned, but Mati was still warned not to let her out of her sight.

All Ivan's powers of persuasion had been needed to get her to wear Ciabhan's ring, and she remained convinced that some great catastrophe had overtaken him. Nothing Ivan said would sway her to believe otherwise. Ivan puzzled over how the ring had managed to come into Leon's possession. He could not believe his friend was dead. He determined that life would go on as before at Compton Berry.

The arrival of Bella Donna allowed Faye to indulge a passion she had long forgone: hawking!

"She is not the best tempered bird," Ivan said, nursing a nasty tear from her beak.

"Then you must learn how to charm this lady, sir!" Faye sympathised, as she wiped blood from his arm with her handkerchief.

"I think it time you wrote again, Faye," he ventured. "You promised it would be finished for your wedding day."

Faye looked at him, perfectly aware of what he was

doing. "Yes, Ivan, you are right. There is still much that I have to include. Tomorrow, I promise, I will spend the day writing. Now, do keep still or she will strike again!"

Her promise to Ivan, however, was forgotten when the day dawned beautiful. On the spur of the moment she decided to take a walk. Mati called after her, "My Lady, where are you going? Wait for me!"

"Fret not, my dear, I am just taking some air before I start the day. Prepare my desk. I will be no more than an hour."

Mati saw her cross the bailey and walk under the oak. Beside her loped the wolfhound, Lupo. Grey and shaggy, he nearly dwarfed her. Faye patted him as they disappeared into the field that led to the lane below the castle. Mati hesitated, remembering Ivan's words. Should she go after her mistress? Surely she would be safe for an hour, and she had Lupo with her. "Madam," she called out, "take care, and don't go too far!"

Lupo panted along beside her, but at times he would run ahead and disappear for a few minutes, always coming back to her side, keeping pace until something else took his interest. Leaving the fields, she met the track that wound down into the town – not the main route used by most travellers and carts, but one the villagers would use when gathering berries. She hadn't intended to walk very far, but before long she found herself heading towards the old Saxon fort that stood on a hill overlooking the river valley. She called Lupo, but again he was far ahead, disappearing over the low wall into the fort. By the time she climbed the steep incline, he was already on the ramparts. His tongue lolling from his mouth, he lay waiting for her at the top of a steep flight of steps.

"Come, boy, we must be getting back. Mati will be fretting." Resting awhile she sat with the dog, lazily stroking his matted coat. "Well, my scruffy friend, we have a fair walk back. What say you we start now?"

A heavy sigh shuddered through his body as he sank his head onto giant crossed paws.

The morning was getting hot, and there was little air. Idly she wandered the walls, gazing over the cottages clustered beneath the fortifications. Out and over the countryside her eyes traced the route she'd taken. Somewhere, deep in the valley towards Compton Berry, lay the magical glade. She wondered if other lovers knew of it.

Two hooded monks in black strolled along the cobbled path that wound its way past the fort. Headed towards the great sandstone church, they sat quietly awhile in the shelter of the guildhall.

Faye felt a wet nose nuzzle her hand and she bent to pat Lupo. When she looked again the seat was empty and the two monks were nowhere to be seen. The silence was broken only by the cawing of a solitary crow. He skimmed the tops of a row of elms that bordered the river in the valley. Like a mirror, the River Dart shone between the trees, curving its glassy way to the sea. Glinting on her finger in the sunlight, the emerald reminded her of Ciabhan and she gazed deep into its green centre, hoping to see his face in the dark, mysterious depths.

"Here, Lupo!" she commanded, taking care with the steps. "Time to go, my friend, or we will be in trouble with Mati."

Increasingly concerned for her mistress's whereabouts, Mati set about finding her. Sending Torr to scour the lanes around Compton Berry, she slipped down to the stream, making a conscious effort to avoid Ivan.

Lapping gently under the willows, the water rippled from the dozens of insects that skipped and plopped onto its surface. Long strands of willow swished against her as Mati pushed the branches aside. With no signs that anyone had been there recently, she stood in the shade unsure where Faye could have gone. A little comfort came from knowing that Lupo was with her.

Ivan's voice shattered the peace. Raised and commanding, it carried through the trees, its brittleness a sure sign of his impatience. Mati heard her name called and prepared to meet his fury. For a few moments more she searched, hoping for a glimpse of Faye's blue frock, but nothing but the breeze stirred. Puffing with exertion, she clambered back through the tangle to be greeted by an angry Ivan on an even angrier beast that snorted and stamped in unison with its master's ill temper.

Edgily he spoke to her: "Good God, madam! This past hour have I searched for you and, more to the point, for your mistress. Where is she?"

Mati stammered a reply: "She wanted to take some air, sir!"

Fixing her with his black eyes, he enquired coldly, "And did you not remember what I asked of you?" He wrestled with the agitated horse, pulling on the reins.

"Yes, sir."

She looked at the ground guiltily, as he berated her. "The fool you call husband was found looking for your mistress on the road to Pagons Ton! Think on it, woman! Is it likely she would be heading in the direction of her husband?" Leaning from the saddle, he hissed, "Pray no harm has come to her, madam!" He whirled in a cloud of dust, the guard clattering after him.

Torr choked as he whispered hoarsely, "That fancy knight had better watch his back, wife! I am no minder to Faye of Pagons Ton. Her place is with her husband!"

Irritated by her husband's malice, Mati said, "Quiet, fool, he is mindful only of our lady's safety."

"Your lady. Make no mistake, madam, she is not mine," he spat.

Faye decided to take the busier cart route back. Had she intended to come into the town she would have brought some money for a drink. She could almost taste Mati's delicious lemon water, as she realised suddenly just how long she had been out. Making her way down the steep street she tried not to linger over the stalls, as Lupo sniffed out almost every cottage entrance.

Just before crossing the bridge, a kindly butcher threw a morsel to the cheeky dog, and Lupo skulked ahead of her with the chunk of offal firmly clamped in his jaws.

She greeted a few familiar faces. A brother from the abbey recognised her from her visit with Ivan, and very politely asked after her well-being and that of Ivan.

Once over the bridge, the track climbed steeply, flattening out at the top, giving Faye a chance to catch her breath. After a brisk walk of about five minutes, the road took a left fork into another rutted cart track as it headed towards Compton Berry.

Faye had just passed the cottage that stood on the division of the road, when the commotion of a group of riders headed in her direction broke the calm of the afternoon. The dust being thrown up suggested they were riding hard, and the horses' hooves could be plainly heard pounding the dry earth. Tucking herself safely into the hedgerow, she prepared for their passing as Lupo came flying back and stood panting by her skirts.

A voice she knew before seeing the speaker halted the riders in a cloud of dirt and grit. Faye held her hands to her face for protection.

"At last, Faye! What in God's name possessed you to disappear with no word to anyone?" His words were harsh. The cloud cleared to reveal the unmistakable shape of Ivan.

Even with the sun behind him and his features in shadow, Faye could tell that he was an angry man, and his tone put her on the defensive. "I did not realise, sir, that I had to ask your permission to walk awhile. Did you think me perhaps headed to Pagons Ton?"

Her sarcasm irritated Ivan. Reaching down, he held out his hand for her to mount behind him. "Do not bandy words with me, madam. Danger stalks these roads. I care only for your safety. Now come, take my hand!"

"Your concern could be better placed, sir. You are mistaken. I need no escort to find my way back to Compton Berry!"

The group sat impassively on restless horses, and tried to look indifferent to the power struggle taking place in front of them.

Ivan, tolerance exhausted, dismounted and took her arm, firmly but gently. Walking her out of earshot, he quietly said, "Mount of your own free will, madam, or by God, I will lift you myself, dignity unguaranteed! The decision is yours, Faye!" The resolve in his voice was clear.

Once in the saddle he again held his hand out to help her. Faye ignored the gesture and without a word pulled herself up sullenly, settling uncomfortably behind him.

Leading the group, he turned the impatient horse in the direction of home. The only time Faye touched him was to steady herself; then she held his waist to stop from falling. Fields and hedgerows passed in a haze of angry tears. They stung her cheeks, adding to her humiliation, but she tried to keep them hidden. This perfect day had now been ruined by Brother Ivan.

Faye did not stop to speak to Mati, who was waiting anxiously at the gate. She slid quickly from the horse's back and rushed past.

Ivan, still in the saddle, watched her disappear through the opening. Bemused, he spoke to Mati: "Methinks the lady needs some time to cool her bad humour, mistress. If she seeks me, I am in the chapel."

In her solar, Faye gave way to her fury. Pacing the floor, she spoke half to Mati, half to herself, asking why? "He commanded me, Mati! He demanded my return. He gave me no choice! Why? How have I angered him?"

Mati tried to calm her mistress, hating to see her so. "I think Brother Ivan was just concerned for your safety, my dear. Danger lurks where you least expect."

"But, from whom?" said Faye, opening her arms and gazing around, genuinely perplexed.

Mati hesitated before speaking. "Leon, maybe?"

Faye stopped pacing. Little creases gathered on her forehead as she pondered this, disbelieving at first, then accepting of the possibility. "Leon? He is spiteful and vindictive, maybe, but think you he would do me harm?"

Mati stared at the ground, and nodded.

"God in heaven!" Faye gasped as she slumped on the cushioned window seat. She reflected on the day's events, and the suggestion that Leon really did mean her harm. Ill-equipped to cope with this, she suddenly felt very alone and vulnerable. She closed her eyes; a timid breeze blew through the open window. Low in the valley it ruffled the trees, and in her mind's eye she pictured the dark place where she and Ciabhan had entered the woods on that magical day. She pictured the owl that slept under the old roof, but suddenly her mind took a dark turn and she imagined the man she loved, lifeless and alone beneath the dank and sodden turf. These black, uninvited thoughts upset her and she shivered as her eyes fell to the emerald flashing in her lap. Ciabhan would never have parted with this ring and panic rose in her throat. She wrapped her arms around herself. Sinking her head onto her chest, she wept stinging tears. "Please, God, don't let our dreams end like this."

A knock sounded and Mati went to the door.

Faye looked up. "I'm not ready to see Ivan yet, Mati!" she said.

Obediently, Mati did as Faye asked, telling him that Faye was sleeping. "Then tell Faye that I will see her at dinner," he said as Mati closed the door.

Faye did not go down to dinner, and when food was sent up it was refused.

Much later, after lighting the candles in the chapel, Ivan went again to see Faye. Hopefully, she would have calmed down. His own frustration was spent; it was time now for talk. Of course, he understood that her pride had been wounded, but Faye was a reasonable woman – she would understand his fears once he explained. Through the arrow slits bright stars lit the heavens and he lingered, fascinated by the shooting stars that seemed to fall to earth. He likened their beauty to that of a woman – fleeting and capricious! With a lighter heart and a smile, Ivan climbed the stairs to Faye's solar, thankful that he had not yet succumbed to the fickle affections of the fairer sex!

Ciabhan knew what he was doing when he left Ivan to care for the beauty he was now on his way to see; it was thanks to God that he possessed the patience of a saint.

Fighting back the depression that had threatened, Faye began to write as she had intended in the first place, remaining at her desk until it was too dark to continue. Pleased with her efforts, she now prepared for bed. Mati brushed Faye's hair in the dimpsy light. The night was balmy, and night sounds drifted through the open window. Sizzling in the grate, a few embers gave a comforting glow to the room, a small flame bringing a flush to the women's faces as they engaged in light-hearted conversation.

Neither heard the latch on the door, or the swish of the visitor's long cloak. Both jumped with shock when Ivan spoke: "I did knock, ladies. My apologies for startling you, but the door was unlocked. If you are busy, I will go." He hesitated, waiting to be asked to stay.

In mock horror, Faye looked around the room, then spoke with exaggerated fear while Mati suppressed a giggle. "Why, sir! Are we in danger of being abducted?"

Ivan, unamused, responded to her comment with dignity. "Sarcasm does not become you, madam!" Turning to Mati, he asked politely, "Please leave us, Mati! I wish to speak with Faye in private."

Faye, still on the defensive, said, "I have no secrets from Mati, sir! She stays!"

As if dealing with a mischievous child, Ivan sighed with exasperation. Moving closer to Faye, he said, "And I keep no secrets from you, which is why I am here! Now leave us, Mati!" His tone was serious now, and Mati left quickly.

Once the door had closed, Ivan crossed to the window. The light from the fire gave his fine features lustre, and his profile flickered clearly on the wall. A moth, drawn to the light, fluttered its dangerous path around the candle flame.

Ivan spoke slowly: "You should be aware that Leon made a threat against you – a threat that I took seriously enough to be concerned for your safety. If I was overzealous in acting to protect you, I apologise." Turning to face her he continued: "I hope that clears up any misunderstanding between us."

Humbled, she answered shamefacedly, "I think, Brother Ivan, that it is I who owe you an apology."

With still no word from Ciabhan, even his friend found it hard to remain positive. Believing there could be many reasons for the lack of news, Ivan was increasingly concerned. He and Faye had made peace, and she agreed enthusiastically when he suggested she learn the basics of self-defence. Ciabhan and Ivan were superb swordsmen, their skills keeping them alive. Ciabhan's life had depended on his expertise as a warrior; treachery alone could bring this knight down. Accustomed to the evil worked by some men, Ivan remained convinced that treachery was indeed at work here; but these thoughts he kept to himself.

Armed with a short sword and small weapons, Faye's first steps into self-defence consisted of little more than familiarising herself with them, and observing Ivan as he went through moves and tactics with guards and volunteers. Later she engaged in actual swordplay, and the art of close combat became clearer.

"Concentrate, Faye, on your enemy's eyes," he warned. "Watch his eyes!" He held her close as they circled their opponent. "Just a flicker could give his next move away, then you act on it! Like this!" He lunged forward – his opponent had allowed his eyes to flicker away for a second. Ivan slashed sideways, twisting her side with his speed but stopping inches from the guard's body. Too late, the guard had jumped back. Ivan, triumphant, said, "That would have stopped him only, not killed him, giving you time to reposition or deal a death blow, like this!" He went on to demonstrate.

Faye replied in gasps as she bent double, winded. "I think I would not have the strength, sir, to deal this death blow," she stammered.

"You will, Faye. You will when your life depends on it!"

He plunged his sword into the soft earth and helped her to her feet. "Up now, madam, quickly! Hesitate, and our opponent would have despatched us both by now!"

He thrust the sword back into her hand as she stammered, trying to straighten, "You are a hard taskmaster, Brother!"

Rain over the next week turned the ground slippery, but the lessons continued.

"Good!" Ivan said. "Understanding the ground beneath your feet could mean the difference between life and death."

With Ivan's coaching and patience she was able to cut and thrust with confidence. To sharpen her reflexes, Ivan picked partners to engage her in mock swordplay. His order was always the same: "Do not go easy on her! Too simple and she will not learn!"

The good-looking Ivan then became a fighting man. He adopted a new persona as one would don a cloak. It was an Ivan Faye could never reconcile, for she could never visualise him as a cold-hearted killer. It even crossed her mind that he delighted in getting his own back on her skittishness.

"Come on, My Lady!" he would goad. Imagine I have just mortally wounded one you love!" The inference was enough to provoke her and, springing at him in a fury of hacks and slashes, she would attack him with genuine anger. "I think, Faye, that Ciabhan would be even more enamoured of you for this defence of his honour!" he would declare playfully as his wiry body backed away from her lunges. Always controlled, his movements by no means lacked grace. A step backwards would never falter or stumble. It seemed to her that invisible hands guided his steps.

Keeping her eyes on his, she held the blade tip just in front of his eyes, barely moving it from side to side, waiting for the flicker of distraction. "And I think, sir, that death should be your reward for such taunts!" she would retort, breathlessly pushing him back.

If by a miracle she ever managed to back him into surrender, he would concede the struggle to her, but far too often he would slide cleverly from her onslaught and evade the final thrust. When the effort was too much for Faye, she would throw down her sword and yield. Although Ivan became used to her wiles, there had been moments of sweet revenge.

Slyly she would feign injury and, as he bent to aid her, she would wriggle out of reach, jumping quickly to her feet. By the time he realised her ruse, she would be standing over him sword to his neck, victorious! "Now, sir, you are at my mercy! What price your life?"

Ivan was rarely caught more than once. At times in the heat of the game, scuffles ended with their weary bodies pushed against each other. They would pull apart shyly, avoiding each other's eyes.

When the ground became too waterlogged and the green in front of the glassy wet walls was a morass of sticky mud and dung, Faye and Ivan moved inside. The clash of metal could be heard all over the castle; from hall and chamber and narrow passageways it ricocheted.

Wisely or not, Faye slept with a dagger beneath her pillow. Leon had given her a dagger many years ago. Like a little toy, its hilt gleamed with mother-of-pearl and cornelian. Next to the glass bird it had lain on the window sill in the house in Pagons Ton. The irony of having to use it to protect herself from the man who gave it to her was not lost on her.

Ivan helped hone her skills with the weapon. He demonstrated the art of inflicting deep, clean cuts for the kill, or bloody gashes that left enemy's flesh torn. Ivan possessed a Sicilian stiletto – a particularly vicious knife. During one session, when he had held her close to demonstrate its uses, an unfortunate move resulted in a cut across three of Faye's fingers. Apologetically, Ivan had lifted her open palm to his mouth and, in a gesture of incredible familiarity, he had kissed the blood away before binding the wound with linen torn from his shirt. Stunned by this intimacy, she was overcome by a sudden and terrible ache as her lips craved the taste of his.

The impulsiveness of the situation seemed to confuse Ivan, and he dropped her hand. With the taste of blood still on his lips, he murmured, "A scratch only, madam! You will live. We will practise no more with this today." His hand shook as he tucked the stiletto into his belt, and he whispered, both avoiding the other's eyes, "Weapons for assassins only, not for play between friends!"

Faye wrestled with the demons of longing as the pit of her stomach somersaulted with an unexpected desire.

Ivan excused himself and left.

That night the tenderness of Ivan's lips on her skin haunted her dreams. Try as she might, she could not shut them out. Desire washed over her body, touching hidden depths. Swimming in its delights, hot and restless, she woke before dawn.

On the floor her nightgown was in a crumpled heap. Pushing the bedcover from her body she allowed the thoughts of long-forgotten passion to flow over her nakedness. The sun, as it rose, drew warm fingers across her burning skin.

So exciting had been the sword lessons that Faye severely neglected her writing. Her story should have ended with the recovery of Ciabhan and their future together, but she had been unaware of his intention to journey to Rome, until the day he broke the news to her. His leaving had caused other situations to occur, and she worried over including the turmoil this parting had caused to her continuing life at Compton Berry. To conclude on a happy note would have been preferable, but she wanted to tell the truth.

With these thoughts in mind, she determined to spend some days writing, catching up with her recollections. It helped that the weather continued to be inclement; murky days when drizzly rain misted the woods became heavy downpours by night. Dampness seemed to creep into the bones, and joints became stiff and achy, especially with the strenuous exercise that had been her regime during these past weeks. Somehow life had become a little more complex since the winter months; she sensed a shift in the relationship between her and Ivan – something intangible, but there nevertheless. Unsettlingly, she felt that he was aware of it also. These were good reasons for putting a little space between them now, providing an opportunity for putting pen to paper once more.

Wrapped warmly, she sat where the light filtered weakly and she could see the grey skies. She began to write.

"I swear it's more like November than late May," she said to Mati. "Ask Torr to build up a fire, please. I will be here all day."

The dread of what had befallen Ciabhan sliced through her raw soul with every word she wrote. Like the swords that had slashed, fear tore into her, hurting far more than the puny scratches from those blades. If Ciabhan was dead, she would wish those swords had killed her.

"This is all so pointless, Mati! He is dead, I am convinced of it!" With rising hysteria she buried her head in her hands and began to sob.

Trying to raise Faye's spirits with words that came far from easily, Mati offered consoling words: "If Brother Ivan says he is alive, believe him, Faye. Listen to his wisdom and be strong! It will be less painful for us all."

Fit, healthy and well up to the challenges of the journey, the four comrades made good travelling time overland from Rome. Leaving Italy, the weather was fair and warm, with spring established, as always, well before that in England. The hardest test should come as they negotiated the *Alpes Maritimus*.

Ciabhan was a happy man. Everything he had requested of the Church had been granted, and Faye was now a free woman. Liberated from the bonds of marriage to a man who cared not for her, she was free to become his spouse. Whether Leon hurt or not was of no consequence to him; he thought only of Faye and he was counting the days to seeing her again. God! how he had missed her! He looked down at the ring – loose now, it twisted on his finger. Hard riding and a meagre diet had toned him, causing a little weight loss.

Keeping to the foothills of the range, with the great Middle Sea to their left, they wound steadily westward to England; the journey's end was in sight.

Before taking the coast road they halted at an isolated hostel, where they had passed a night on the way out. Run-down and not very clean, it nevertheless served good food and untainted wine and provided fine cover for the horses.

After a hearty meal and plenty of local wine, Ciabhan and Alain slept unusually soundly. The Turks, who abstained totally from alcohol, drank only water but they later recalled an unnatural drowsiness. They remembered nothing until they woke well into mid-morning, hours past their normal rising time. An eerie stillness hung over the inn. Sounds one would expect to hear were missing – no voices or animal noises broke the strange quiet! All life seemed to have vanished into thin air.

Warily they looked about them, slowly comprehending the reality of the situation. All their possessions had gone – horses, baggage and weapons! Nothing remained. During the hours of darkness and with incredible stealth, everything had been removed while they had all slept on. It would have been so easy to murder them so why such trouble to delay their journey only?

Bewilderment gave way to rage when Ciabhan discovered the precious emerald ring was missing from his finger. Pacing the ground furiously, he invoked all the saints in heaven. In disbelief he studied the pale band where only a few hours ago the ring had glinted against bronzed skin. How in God's name had that been removed without his awareness? Why had reflexes, usually so sharp, failed him? The fleeting thought crossed his mind that so easily his finger or his whole hand could have been lost! Maybe they had been lucky, after all! Confused, he stumbled as he looked around at the empty buildings, apparently devoid of any life.

A dishevelled and equally puzzled Alain joined him, unnerved as the truth slowly began to dawn. In the hush of midday as the sun warmed baked hills, Alain spoke: "Sir, it is not hard to see evil at work here. Ours was no natural sleep, and someone has taken great trouble and risk to hinder our journey home, yet not kill us. As to the reason, my friend, I haven't a clue!"

With only the clothes they stood in – no money, weapons or baggage – Ciabhan and Alain discussed with their two companions the best way to continue their journey. They agreed to head for Aquitaine, Alain's homeland.

"Once we are there, my family will offer all we require in order to continue, sir."

Ciabhan still paced the ground, seething. Blaming himself for their predicament, his companions could say nothing that would lighten his load, and he fussed constantly over his ringless finger. The theft of the emerald separated him from Faye, cutting him off from the woman he loved – the woman he was returning to marry. He smacked his fist into his palm, his eyes ablaze with determination. "No common thief keeps me from my wedding day, sirs! Are you with me?"

In accord, his companions yelled their support, while Alain clasped his hand. "I think that is a resounding yes, My Lord."

Luck was with them as they found shelter and sanctuary in religious institutions such as monasteries. Most had heard of Ciabhan of Compton Berry. Gifts and charity from sympathisers saw them gain transport, loans and weapons.

On reaching the borders of Aquitaine, they once again had all they needed. Alain's hometown welcomed them as heroes, believing them returning from war. As a son of Aquitaine, Alain was afforded the honours of a homecoming crusader. They were given shelter and provisions aplenty for the journey to England.

Ciabhan, with great diplomacy, gave Alain the choice of staying with his parents in the small but comfortable town of his birth.

Without hesitation, and true to his oath of allegiance, Alain swore to follow Ciabhan wherever the path of loyalty took him. "I chose to follow you, sir, and my mind has not changed. I will honour my oath."

It was with gladness that Ciabhan embraced the young knight, promising his saddened parents that he would care for him as a son. While his mother clung to her embarrassed son weeping softly, Ciabhan spoke gently to her: "Fear not for your son, madam, for he is as dear to me as to yourselves."

Mati had loved Sir Ciabhan from the moment she first set

eyes on him in the courtyard of the house in Pagons Ton. He, of course, had eyes for none but his lovely hostess and their game of one-upmanship. Mati had witnessed the near unhorsing of the Templar that day.

Her husband, Torr, had remarked sourly then, "Master Leon had better look to his wife! This Templar has been long on the road!"

Irritated with her husband's hatred of the Templars, and for some reason this one in particular, she had answered him through gritted teeth, "Quiet, husband, or you might find that bitter tongue removed from your mouth one of these days!"

Mati had served Faye some time before marrying Torr, the reeve of Leon's manor. Theirs had been a hastily arranged marriage with Mati already carrying Torr's child. The loveless match, however, benefited them both in social status – a husband-and-wife team providing support for their master and his lady. The union had produced an only child – a son.

At his wife's rebuke, Torr had slunk off, muttering.

Before her like a God shone Ciabhan, but not as much as a glance even passed in her direction, captivated as he was by the Lady Faye. Instantly, he had been a focus of fantasy for Mati; silent dreams had helped her to accept the misery of her marriage. Realistic enough to know that for Ciabhan she barely existed, she carried an invisible torch for him from that moment onward. Selflessly she served Faye, sharing heartaches and confidences. Faye, in return, put the interests of her loyal young maid and her family high on her list of priorities, caring for her greatly.

Torr, on the other hand, seethed with resentment. Torn from Leon by events out of his control, he eventually found himself at Compton Berry. The intrigues of the Templar had ruined his cosy life with Leon in Pagons Ton, just as predicted. He now lived courtesy of a man he hated – and worse, he suspected that his own wife had fallen under the spell of Sir Ciabhan of Compton Berry. Little affection towards him, unreasonable tears, and Mati's increasingly bad humours pointed all too clearly to this.

One morning he declared to his snivelling wife and small son, "I am thinking of moving us south, wife. The boy will be able to work soon, and I have enough put aside for a smallholding."

His words made Mati's blood run cold. The thought of being away from all she loved at Compton Berry terrified her. This must be a ploy by Torr to distance her from her mistress, she thought. She would avoid saying anything to Faye, whose mental state was fragile enough – she would stay silent and hope Torr would change his mind. The less time spent in his presence the better, she resolved.

Mati was glad Faye had decided to spend a few days quietly writing; it would be a period for reflection and calm as they went about their chosen tasks.

As the days of rain wore on, Faye's spirit became restless. Stopping her writing, she would pace the room as if thinking. Mati stayed silent, speaking only when spoken to.

On this particular afternoon, Faye flung open the window and put her head out. The wind whipped her hair across her skin in damp strands. The valley was quiet as the rain skimmed across the trees, and she wondered if anyone moved through their waterlogged depths. She leant further, looking down the wall, her fingers gripping the slimy stones. Without any warning, she caught the glint of the emerald as it slid slowly from her finger. Winking brightly at her, as if glad to be free, it spun down against the dark barricade, landing in a clump of stinging nettles at the base of the wall. Horrified, she called Mati. "Oh, my God, Mati, the ring! It's fallen from my finger. It's an omen! Oh, my God, it's an omen! I knew it! Ivan's wrong – Ciabhan's dead." Faye ran from the solar. "I must find it. I must, or all will be lost – even my sanity!"

Beneath the walls with her bare hands she pulled at the clumps of nettles. Viciously they stung her, but feeling nothing she continued to scrabble at the roots. Ivan, having witnessed her flight, caught up with the two women as they searched on their hands and knees. Faye was almost hysterical.

"In God's name, what goes on here?" he said, bemused.

Mati answered him: "The ring, sir, the ring! Ciabhan's ring – it slid from Faye's finger."

Ivan gently raised Faye. Forlornly she looked at him as he said, "Be assured, Faye, it will be found. Now I suggest you wash the mud from your hands and your gown before it is ruined!"

The little chapel was cool as Ivan knelt in front of his altar. A profound peace ruled within these walls and wrapped around him. He loved its sanctuary. The chapel sat above the great gate and looked out over the entrance to the castle. Directly beneath the chapel was the guardroom, and voices would sometimes drift up into the quiet. Religious scenes in bright colours decorated the walls, while the ceiling was a warming shade of terracotta. As a reminder of Ciabhan's devotion to the Christian cause, his shield hung on the wall over the table where candles were placed to shine for its absent owner. Battered, the red cross bore the scars of battle. Ivan would run his fingers along the cuts and tears on its surface, and remember his friend.

Opposite the entrance, a narrow passage led off from the chapel. Two rooms only could be accessed from this: one was Ivan's and the other Ciabhan's. To the left, down a steep flight of stairs was Ivan's; small and sparsely furnished, it reflected his basic needs. A large wooden crucifix hung at the head of his bed. The limited space allowed for only a clothes stand, escritoire and small altar. Along the passageway to the right, at the top of two flights of narrow stairs, Ciabhan's chamber overlooked the whole of the castle.

Still on his knees, Ivan studied the emerald ring in his hand. Washed free of the mud that had encrusted it, the troublesome jewel rested, beautiful in his palm. What pain this innocent gem had caused its wearers! It lay benignly in Ivan's grasp and he pondered if it were not a bad talisman, for it seemed to have brought nothing but sorrow to all who had possessed it. Maybe he should lie and tell Faye that its retrieval had eluded him! Shamed by such a thought, he was unaware of Faye; the sweep of her skirts on the flagstones took him by surprise. Rising from his knees, he greeted her by taking her hand and placing the ring once more on her finger, smiling at her joy.

He remained motionless as she embraced him, whispering her thanks: "Dear Ivan, I can never thank you enough."

Releasing her arms gently from his neck, the closeness of her body almost too much to bear, he replied, "It's enough for me that you are happy, Faye. Now I have duties to attend to."

She hesitated but did not leave, choosing instead to light a candle. Her hand shaking slightly, she said, "I came to light a candle for Ciabhan. I did not expect to see you here, Brother. I thought you asleep." She placed the candle in a holder on the votive table, where its little flame flickered brightly beneath the red and white shield. "Will you join me in a prayer for My Lord, Ivan?"

Side by side they knelt at the altar, each absorbed in their own special prayers. Twilight descended dimming the painted room; figures on the walls seemed to move as the dancing flames gave them life. Outside, dusk turned the evening sky deep blue, and tiny bats flitted across treetops hunting in the evening balm. Faye sat with head bowed, quietly meditating as Ivan continued his duties. Safe within the familiarity of its walls, the chapel offered welcome respite and peace for her as well as for Ivan, and she remembered his unwillingness to allow fighting here. It was the only place in the whole castle where he had forbidden any swordplay whatsoever.

Her prayers for Ciabhan complete, Faye rose to go. "Thank you again, Ivan, for taking the time to find the ring. I will sleep a little easier tonight."

She bent in front of the altar and genuflected.

Her reluctance to leave alone was obvious and Ivan asked her quietly, "Would you like me to accompany you, Faye?"

Her voice trembled a little as she replied, "I would like that very much."

As Ivan followed her to the door, he noticed the creamy

skin of the back of her neck, just visible through the loose strands of hair before she pulled her hood over her head. As always, he left the door unlocked for any who may wish to enter and pray and for his return later.

Faye asked as he left the door ajar, "Is it wise to leave the door unlocked, sir?"

A flush had crept up from her neck over her cheeks turning their cream to a soft rose as he answered her:"No thieves dwell among us here, Faye, but there are those that pray."

In silence they climbed the stairs to Faye's solar. With every step Ivan's head pounded. He wanted to flee, to turn back to the sanctuary of his chapel, but desire had him in its grip. He hesitated once more, but Faye's perfume filled his senses – like a magnet, it pulled him after her!

A small coloured lantern cast a saffron glow over the pale linen covers, and delicate embroidery decorated the plump pillows that lay against the bedhead, which was carved with roses and acorns. Ivan had never noticed the bed until this moment, although he had been in this chamber before. His eyes alighted on two items in particular: a footstool at the bottom of the bed had been covered with a woven tapestry of a blood-red cross on a white background – a Templar cross for Ciabhan – woven with love, and a cross carved into the oak wood of the bedhead. It was a reminder that this bed had belonged to Ciabhan.

Any second thoughts Ivan had about this moment were forgotten as Faye turned her lovely face to him. By the light her features were ethereal, and she shone like the faery women she was named after.

With her finger on her lips, she whispered, "I think we are alone." She walked through the small inner room as if someone might be there, removing the light wrap from her shoulder as she went.

Ivan glimpsed more of the honeyed skin he had so wanted to caress. That was the moment he should have listened to his head and gone. Yes, she might have hurt, but their honour would have been intact. Now there was no going back – the die was cast!

She returned, satisfied that they were alone. "Do you wish to stay, Ivan?"

The moment was finally lost when he turned and shot the heavy bolt across the door, locking them away from the world. Seconds later he was kissing the woman he had desired for so long. Faye returned his kisses with equal intensity; the weeks of craving were at last satisfied.

When their lips were finally apart, Ivan gasped, "For this moment, Faye, I would have walked barefoot in fire."

In seconds, the bed yielded to the forbidden lovers.

Faye sighed, "For this moment, Ivan, I already burn with guilt; the fire of passion consumes me."

As if untying the most precious of gifts, Ivan took the clothes slowly from Faye's body. Tremors of pleasure shivered through her skin as she lay naked at last beneath his gaze. He ran his elegant hands the length of her body, feeling the dips and valleys of every curve. Feverishly, Faye tossed her head from side to side. With little moans, she arched her back as, straddling her, he wrapped his arms around her waist, lifting her convulsing body tight to his. His head lay on her breasts as, tenderly kissing and sucking them, he moved his tongue the length of her body. All the time with words of love he confessed his adoration of her, and slowly, slowly, as her honey flowed, he took her to heaven.

"Yes, sweet Faye, just for you! This is just for you. Take what you must of me and enjoy it, my love!"

Faye writhed with absolute pleasure. Her abandonment was total as Ivan moaned that paradise could not better this moment. Stroking her hair, he watched as ecstasy shuddered through her, making her cry out. Three times they consumed each other that night. Damp with sweat they writhed, his golden skin and hers, paler, entwined together, they exhausted each other with their passionate love-making.

Just before the first cock crowed, Ivan gathered his clothes and made a hushed exit. Bending over the still-sleeping Faye, he kissed her forehead. She smiled a secret smile, stretched and turned onto her back as if to welcome his new embrace, but slept on. Arranging the crumpled coverlet over her naked breasts, he gazed on her form beneath the cover. Never would he see her like this again, and he wanted to remember the woman who had given him the gift of her body – the woman he would love as long as he lived, even though in her moment of ecstasy it was Ciabhan's name she had called.

"God forgive me," he whispered, crossing himself.

Not noticing the emerald on the floor, his foot just missed kicking it as he left the room. As Faye had surrendered to her passion, the already loose ring had flown from her finger, fracturing the once flawless stone. Absorbed in their love-making, neither had heard the crack as the heavy ring hit the wall and fell to the floor, a silent witness of betrayal.

By the half-open door, Torr's shadowy form seemed huge. Mati, only semi-awake, was restless in the bed as he mumbled, "Wake up, wife, and listen to your perfect mistress! It would appear she is getting somewhat more of the Raven than is usual! I wonder that you slept through it!" Mati sat up and listened as Torr carried on, his tone scornful: "Can you not hear how the lady cries out like a whore? Methinks the Raven would do well to gag his noisy paramour!" The sounds of Ivan and Faye's love-making echoed down the empty stairwell. Bouncing off walls, it rang loud in her reluctant ears. She covered them against its invasion of her mind as Torr continued his tirade: "You can cover your ears, madam, but the truth is there for all to hear!" He pushed her roughly towards the door. "Listen well, wife!"

Clawing at his hands, Mati broke free of her despicable husband and spat at him, "Your mouth is full of poison, like the serpent you are, spewing filthy words of venom! I will listen no longer to such wickedness. Your very presence is loathsome to me!"

"Not as loathsome as the name you sigh for in your sleep night after night, woman. How it sickens me to hear you moan for him! Even now, above our very heads, the Templar's betrothed cuckolds him with his false friend, and you weep for the fool!" He mocked as Mati, distressed, stumbled around the room. "You are pathetic and foolish, wife! Think you that such as Ciabhan of Compton Berry would even look in your direction? Yet you cry into your pillow for him. Did you think me so stupid I would not notice?" Mati whimpered, sinking to the ground while Torr berated her, enjoying her humiliation. "Be assured murder will be on his mind when our Lord of Compton Berry learns of this treachery; what say you, madam? Who do you think will perish first on his sword of revenge? His pride will demand their blood!"

Furious now, Mati hissed at him, "Are you so bitter and evil that even the dead must be spoken of so? Does your malice know no bounds?"

She gasped at his next words: "Dead? Who said he was dead? What if I were to tell you that your fancy knight is but days from these very walls?"

Ciabhan woke with a start. Around him the clearing was quiet; not a leaf rustled or animal stirred. In its circle of stones the embers smouldered in the night's still air.

The nightmare had left him in a sweat so real that it had been more like an apparition. His eyes fearfully roamed the shadows, half expecting the dream to reappear. Propping himself against the oak stump, he made out the shapes of the Turks in the gloom. Fitfully they slept – nothing had disturbed them. Only Alain, hunched in a blanket, sat apart, his profile clear in the glow of the fire's warmth.

Ciabhan's thoughts raced as his mind cleared; visions came back to haunt him. Even with eyes tightly shut his sight and senses were assailed by the image of Faye, pale and small, her body enfolded in the wings of a raven. Desirous, the creature encircled her nakedness, almost human in its protective stance. The half-open beak resembled a sword, smote in two, ready to defend, but equally capable of great harm. Keenly the raven's jet eyes, deep and unfathomable, scanned the clearing. All around the bird's glossy black head, great emeralds, as large as stones, fell like rain, brilliant green and dramatic against

119

the indigo sky. As is the strange way of dreams, these huge emeralds caused no hurt to either raven or captive as they fell to the ground; a ghostly green light illuminated the whole scene as glittering emeralds slowly and soundlessly covered the ground. Fixed in Ciabhan's mind were Faye's troubled eyes. Wide, they stared from the raven's embrace, and, although not afraid, they were the saddest he had ever seen – eyes seeking something long lost.

The significance of the dream was not lost on Ciabhan. Whether he dozed again after, he did not know, but the darkness gradually lifted from the encampment and birdsong welcomed the new day, chasing away the terrors of the nightmare.

Collecting possessions together, the little group broke camp and breasted the hills heading south. Only Ciabhan seemed strangely disconcerted by the raucous cawing of a solitary crow, spoiling the morning chorus with its harshness as it flew low over their heads. He imagined it would reach its destination long before they reached theirs, and his heart lurched.

On a day of intermittent showers, Ciabhan returned to Compton Berry; barking dogs and excited voices heralded his arrival. The commotion reached Faye's ears first, then Mati appeared in the doorway, a look of utter disbelief on her face.

The unpredictability of the weather had found Faye idling her hours away. Trying to lessen the boredom, she had playfully tormented Ivan as he worked at his desk in a corner of the great hall. Unable to distract him, she had taken up a position in the window recess overlooking the valley and had spent her time gazing over the countryside as the misty drizzle descended once more. Ivan's glossy black hair fell over his eyes. Constantly he swept it back, only for it to flop forward again as if with a mind of its own. The memory of that fateful night, when lust had overtaken common sense, caused her body to tremble still. She recalled his silky hair, falling like curtains around her face, as the Raven had enveloped her body with his desire and they had indulged in a night of intense passion. Again she shivered at the memory.

It was the sound of the dogs that made Ivan look up, dark eyes suddenly expectant. Dropping his quill on the desk, he stood, carelessly knocking over the stool, its clatter filling the room. He ran from the great hall, down the stairs and out into the bailey.

A cursory look only passed between Mati and Faye as she brushed past her maid, but in that look lay a thousand unspoken words! Mati, her mouth open in disbelief, followed her mistress, already on the heels of Ivan.

Ivan was too fast for Faye. Only the slapping of his sandals over the floor sounded in her ears as he flew across the lower rooms and out into the bright light, his black cloak flowing around his brown, hose-free legs.

Suddenly transfixed, Faye stood rooted to the spot. Great tears ran down her face as the emotion of waiting overwhelmed her.

Ciabhan saw only the woman he loved. Already dismounted, he hurried to her, while Ivan ecstatically beamed at his side. Faye stood in a swathe of crumpled green silk. Green! He thought of the colour of the ring – their colour! Sweeping her body into his arms, he held her close, whispering, his lips brushing the tear-streaked cheeks. For a second the sun shone brilliantly from behind the clouds. "No more tears, Faye. No more tears, ever again!"

Bringing us up to the present the story of Faye, Ciabhan and Ivan continues with the approaching wedding day . . . .

Honour lost,
But beauty won.
A lady loved
A knight undone.

To the west a thunderhead loomed; slowly it advanced. Behind its bright edge the sky was brilliant, the silver outline blinding. Gradually the bubbling dark mass pushed the fresher air aside, and replaced it with sticky humidity. It heralded an oppressive night.

Faye had hardly noticed the change in the weather. The hours had crept by and she had stopped only occasionally, too absorbed in her writing to notice the passing of time either.

She jumped with surprise when she heard Ciabhan's soft voice from behind her: "At last, my dear! I thought you would never cease writing. This past hour I have been patiently waiting!" Ciabhan sat against the wall in the shade of the roof overhang. In shadow his skin glowed with health from his day in the sun. His dark-brown eyes were so beautiful in his golden face that Faye thought him the most handsome man on God's earth. He was so perfect that he took her breath away. Casually he sat on the hard floor, arms resting on his knees. In the shadow the emerald flashed, contrasting with the brown of his hands. Playfully he laughed. "I never intended to shock you so, Faye."

Overcome with love for this man, she put down her quill, crossed to him and knelt at his feet. Caressing his hands, she replied, "I can't believe I didn't hear your footsteps, My Lord."

"Are you finished with our tale, madam?" he asked, stroking her hot face.

"No. It is difficult to write about the suffering of the man you love. It has been painful," she answered honestly.

"Write what you must, Faye, for in truth pain played a large part in our story, did it not?"

She nearly drowned in his eyes. Melting in their depths, she rested her face on his strong hands, the veins pulsing as his hot blood coursed through them. In silence they sat thinking as one. Ciabhan bent and kissed her hair as she continued to brush her lips over his fingers.

From the chapel roof a blackbird sang plaintively, and its mate answered from deep in the wood as the first rumble of thunder growled in the ever lowering sky. Around the glistening walls thunder reverberated, and lightning lit the passageways and echoing halls as the castle braved the pounding from the elements. In Faye's chamber the decorative tapestries were brought to life. Pastoral scenes of mountains, rivers and valleys were lit with colour. Blues and greens and blood-red were highlighted by the little coloured glass panes rattling in the window, chasing colours across the hangings. Lakes rippled and trees swayed, but Faye saw none of this.

Huddled beneath the wolfskin on her bed, she cowered as the bats and demons of hell sizzled and flickered across the weavings. Head covered, she tried to blot out the sounds, and the bravado with which she had greeted the early rumblings was long gone. She wished she had asked Mati to stay this night, but had decided against it, insisting that she wanted to carry on writing. So proud had she been of her day's work. With luck she might have it ready to give Ciabhan on their wedding day. Diligently she had written until the light had gone, abandoning it only as the storm broke. Strangely, just before that moment, a few words had flashed into her mind and, unjumbling them, a small verse had formed. Peeping out of the comforting wolfskin, she could see that the little candle flame was still burning, bravely facing the draught that flapped the draperies. Her writing paraphernalia was still on the table; it would take only a few moments. The floor chilled her feet as she dipped quill into ink and wrote quickly before the words vanished from her mind:

TO CIABHAN

Our story, far from being done,
Will live each day, my love, my sun;
And when death calls for us to part,
You'll live for ever in my heart.

Satisfied, she climbed back under the thick fur and slept at last. If she had ventured to the window, she would have seen the havoc below her walls. The inner bailey was awash, and weary men tried desperately to secure all that could move. Soaked to the skin, Ciabhan and Ivan battled alongside man and beast with what seemed like the wrath of the Almighty against them.

The storm grew in intensity and the two friends battled against its force. Above the wind someone screamed in pain. By the time Ivan reached the injured party, his moans of agony were nearly as loud as the storm itself! A piece of falling masonry had struck one of the gate guards. Ciabhan helped Ivan haul the barely conscious man across the quagmire that had been the bailey and into the guardroom.

Skilfully, Ivan patched up the injury before leaving him bloodied but thankful to be alive. The guard weakly smiled his thanks. "He'll live," laughed Ivan at two dishevelled men throwing dice in front of a fire that spat and hissed as the backdraught flung flames against the blackened firewall. "You Devonians have the resilience of oxen!"

The castle shuddered and groaned under the onslaught as it took the full force of the storm's ferocity. Outside, the overladen forest howled as the wind ripped through its heart.

"Aye, sir, especially old Granite Head there!" said one of his companions.

The only light came from the lightning as Ciabhan and Ivan headed through the chapel to their beds. Seeing Faye's room finally in darkness, Ciabhan said, "It seems my lady sleeps at last."

Once in his room, Ciabhan kicked off his boots, and conversed with the young Page waiting with water and oil. "Some storm, lad! Come, help me out of this foul garb!"

Free of his filthy clothes, he cleansed the grime from his body with cool fresh water. Being clean before bed was a luxury Ciabhan insisted on whenever possible. Looking down into the bailey, he drained a cup of mulled wine as lightning illuminated his nakedness.

Marvelling at its awesome might and the fragility of nature, a movement close to the wall caught his attention. The unmistakable figure of Ivan made his way towards the great hall, cloak billowing behind him. A frown crossed Ciabhan's brow as he wondered at his friend's mission –

probably another injury, he thought. It would be a late night for his friend.

Shivering as his body dried in the night air, he slid beneath the heavy fur cover. His thoughts soon turned to Faye – not long now, and he would be holding her in his arms all night long.

The tap on Faye's door was light. From beneath heavy covers she waited again to be sure her ears were not playing tricks; there were so many unfamiliar sounds this terrible night. But again it came, a little louder, more urgent. Who on earth would be calling now? Dragging the covers around her, she padded to the door and pulled back the heavy bolt. The door flew inwards. Half expecting to see Ciabhan, she clasped both hands to her face as Ivan caught her in his arms.

Steadying her, he whispered, "Fear not, Faye."

She stammered in surprise, "So late! Ivan, is there a problem?" Tangled in the covers, she struggled to move.

Ivan bent down and gathered the fabric. Drawing it warmly around her shoulders, he guided her towards the chair by the fire. When settled, he knelt in front of her and with great tenderness drew her hands away from her face. "Faye, I need to talk to you. Please listen." He watched as tears welled to the surface of her eyes, as if she were aware of what he had come to say. She finally looked up at Ivan – the man she and Ciabhan both adored; the man she had betrayed Ciabhan with; his great friend! Her eyes fell on the bed and quickly she looked away. Ivan turned his back on the bed. "Faye, I have come to tell you of my leaving – to prepare you before I tell Ciabhan." He hesitated before continuing: "In a few days I will be gone."

His words took a few moments to sink in. When they did, the tears threatened to spill over. In rivers they ran down her face as the realisation of what he was saying hit her. "Before our wedding?" she sobbed.

"Yes, all the saints in heaven cannot stop my torment. I have tried through prayer but the agony goes on. Each day is worse than the last. I must seek penance. Ciabhan brought word that my mother is not well; if it is not too late already, it would be a fitting time to leave. Ciabhan will understand."

Her rising panic had threatened hysteria, but in her heart she knew his words made sense. Ivan, so assertive and strong, now looked troubled and she couldn't bear to see him suffer. Soothingly she said, "You do not suffer alone, Ivan, for we both endure this burden of guilt. Our shame will fester and eat away at us. If you feel it best to go, then go you must, although my heart will be heavy at your leaving."

The storm continued to rage, and it felt as if God himself raged at them for their betrayal. Ivan wanted to confess his true feelings for her. He could no longer live under the same roof as the woman he loved, and the real reason for his leaving was his continuing desire for her. How could he possibly marry the woman he loved to his dearest friend? It would be easier to lie, break his promise to Ciabhan, and face his disappointment. "I will tell Ciabhan tomorrow," said Ivan.

Faye nodded. "I owe so much to you, dearest Ivan. If you had never come into my life, Ciabhan would have probably died on foreign soil and I, at the mercy of age, would have withered and died. Never would we have known of our love for each other." She reached for the hand of the unshaven and mud-spattered man in front of her. "Nor would I have had the honour of your friendship, for a truer friend never existed. Do what you must, Ivan, but forever you will be in here." She touched her heart.

"And you in mine," he replied, pulling the cover back over her shoulders. He had seen her shiver as the air in the chamber had turned chill. As his fingers touched her icy skin, he was reminded of the one night's weakness that had caused this painful parting. Then her skin had been so hot. Ashamed of even that fleeting thought, he forced himself to speak, the words difficult: "Faye, nothing must come between you and Ciabhan – not us, not remorse, nothing! Fate has decreed your love, and our mistake must not threaten that." His lips brushed her tangled hair. "Now rest. You are cold. Remember all will be well. Try and think upon this night as a bad dream." He left her lit by the retreating storm, a beautiful, pale statue alone with her torment.

The figure lurking in the gloom at the bottom of the stairs moved not a muscle as the Raven slipped past the doorway to Mati's room. Holding his breath until sure Brother Ivan was out of earshot, Torr then smiled, cruelly.

None heard the footsteps cross the chapel floor. Swiftly, with one purpose in mind, they mounted the stairs to the master's high chamber.

Below the chapel Ivan slept exhausted. Had he seen the candle flame flicker on the wall as the shadow passed, he would not have investigated. On a night when even the walls shook, only those that slumbered were still!

The grubby piece of parchment had been swept almost out of sight and lay concealed until Alain, on entering the chamber, pulled the tapestry hanging back from the door. He picked it up and casually handed it to Ciabhan. "Some night, sir! The walls took quite a battering. Ivan's already with the injured. And the oaf who stopped the block lives still!"

Ciabhan, puzzling over the note in his hand, asked, "And Faye?"

Alain replied, noting Ciabhan's puzzled expression, "Fine, sir! Is something wrong?"

The words scrawled across the paper in a spidery hand were brief and a frown creased Ciabhan's forehead: *'Know your nemesis, and look upon the Raven, for in the cracked jewel lies his treachery.'*

Carefully he folded the paper and tucked it into his tunic – strange words indeed! He would study them later. The mud from last night caked his boots and dried bits of earth cracked and fell off as he struggled to pull them on impatiently. Still thinking of the note, he remembered his emerald. The jewel? Was that the jewel? but that was flawless – not a mark on it. Did the note refer to the emerald? The Raven was obviously his friend, and he was no traitor! He remained mystified as to why the emerald had been stolen when they had been robbed, and even more baffled to find it at Compton Berry. Since learning of Leon's threat to Faye, he had suspected him or an accomplice. Man was capable of taking extreme measures to win back an errant wife, or his wounded pride – and puffed with pride Leon the mercenary certainly was.

Nervously Mati straightened her apron as she waited in the great hall. Faye had told her to stay by the desk in the corner where Ivan used to sit in Ciabhan's absence.

It was Ciabhan's habit to consider the tasks of the day while taking breakfast – the only time he could be found alone other than when in his chamber. He came through the door studying a piece of paper. He saw Mati as she stepped aside for him. Puzzled as to why she was there, he looked around then asked, "No problems, I hope?"

She could always tell where Ciabhan had passed because of the rose water he used. Unlike many men, he preferred to smell pleasant. His scent lingered in rooms he had visited, and she would hang back just to savour his presence. She had guarded her secret well, until treacherous dreams had given her away to Torr.

In awe as always of Ciabhan, she hesitated until he spoke to her: "Well, Mati? I have work to do! Is it Faye?"

"No, sir. Faye writes, but it was she who suggested I talk to you."

"Well, mistress, talk then!" he said a little impatiently.

She told him about Torr wanting to take her away from all that she knew. She said she did not want to leave Compton Berry or the mistress she loved, but duty meant she must follow her husband and child; and besides she had no means of her own.

"And your husband? Does he have the means?"

"Yes, sir, and he will take the child."

Normally of good judgment, Ciabhan guessed there was no love between this couple. Straight to the point, he asked, "Do you want to go?"

"No," she stammered.

"Then stay! Consider Compton Berry your home, madam. You are a true and loyal companion to Faye, and she loves you. With or without the child, it is up to you and your husband. Your marital differences are of no interest to me, but consider yourself under my personal protection." Mati squeezed his hand in thanks. Such a show of affection embarrassed him, but he smiled, making her heart leap, even though his next words were curt: "You have my word, woman – let that be enough! There's no need for excessive thanks!"

She lost no time in finding her husband, her mind made up.

Ciabhan had dismissed Mati and her troubles. True, he did not much care for Torr himself, agreeing with both Faye and Ivan that the husband of Mati could do with a lesson in manners and respect. It was for Faye's sake alone that he had offered her maid his protection, and he gave no more thought to the incident. Eager for a day's hunting with Ivan as promised, he hurried outside to the stables.

By the end of the day both were tired, and Ivan had still not found the right moment to tell Ciabhan of his decision to leave; it would have to be sometime before dinner; time was running out. Ciabhan had insisted on showing Ivan something. Now, following him deeper into the wood, Ivan was glad of the slower pace and the shade. Loosening his tunic ties, he mopped the back of his neck. Insects droned by and midges in their thousands rose into the shafts of sunlight as the weary horses ploughed on. Backs steaming, they snorted and tossed their heads free of clouds of gnats.

Ivan watched his friend slash through the vicious brambles, his blade dulled purple with blackberry stains. Over his shoulder, Ciabhan called to Ivan, "Remember, my friend, when I promised we would hunt together in these woods?"

Breaking through the tangle, Ivan shouted back, "How could I ever forget? It was the focus for our return!"

As they broke free of the undergrowth, Ivan was instantly transported back to his childhood by the sight of the clearing in front of him. He remembered the stifling countryside on the outskirts of Rome, when he would give overprotective servants the slip, and, if lucky, hide in the cooling shade of places just like this. For maybe a precious hour he could lie alone, watching the clouds float by while dreaming of the world around him. He had been an inquisitive child, always asking questions, and determined to learn and travel. The household servants had an affectionate name for him: the little dreamer, they had called him.

He gazed as sunbeams towered as tall as the trees, like lucent pillars. Their bases seemed to end in puddles of lime, flooding the ground in bright liquid. "I've never seen a more natural cathedral; it's amazing," he gasped. "Has Faye seen this?" he said.

"Her reaction was much the same as yours. A cathedral she called it also."

They sat quietly for a while, and Ciabhan seemed to take delight in his friend's reaction as he looked around.

When he spoke next, his words were hesitant, almost self-conscious, as if grown men should not feel such sentiment: "This place is special to Faye and me. After our wedding, I plan to restore the lodge as a place of sanctuary – a gift for her. She knows nothing of my plans; you are the only one I have told. You will help me, of course, my friend?"

Seconds passed before Ivan blurted out the lie he immediately regretted: "My Lord, I have been tardy in telling you, for I have not had the opportunity, but I must leave before your wedding day. I have received unexpected news from my father. I have no choice. I was going to tell you this evening!"

Shafts of sunlight captured Ciabhan in misty gold and silver, as columns of light appeared to imprison him in their midst. Reminiscent of an ancient temple, the image hung between reality and dream, while from its middle Ciabhan shone like one of the heroes of old – the same Ciabhan whose magnetism had held Ivan in thrall from the first moment he had seen him. If he had been taken aback by Ivan's words, he did not show it! Rather, his composure was uncannily cold, the radiance about him at odds with his next words. Humbly he pleaded, "We have planned for this day so long, my friend. Without you to marry us, Faye will be a most unhappy bride! Our day will be incomplete. I would not stand between you and your familial duty, sir, but a few days only, Ivan? Just for the ceremony? Then go as you must with our blessing."

In turmoil, Ivan's throat tightened and his heart thumped loudly in his chest. How could he in honour marry the woman he loved to the man he so venerated. This surely was the Almighty moving in mysterious ways. He and Faye, it seemed, had been called to face their demons. What fools they had been to think it could ever have been otherwise!

Nothing stood in Ciabhan's way once his mind had been made up, and seeing Ivan's hesitation he continued: "I will ask nothing more of you, Ivan; but will you do it for Faye?"

With such a plaintive plea, Ivan could hardly deny his friend on such a special day – he had, after all, made the promise. "Forgive me for even thinking otherwise," he said. "How could I have even considered not being here for you both? My words were uttered in haste; the letter has been a shock! I will leave the day after."

Ciabhan, no longer godlike but human and grateful, gripped Ivan's hands. "I will never forget this, Ivan; I am in your debt."

The younger man could barely contain his shame. Battling silently with his guilty conscience, he bit down hard on his lips to stop the words from escaping, managing only a weak smile of acceptance.

Earlier in the morning, when alone together by the stables, Ciabhan had shown Ivan the note, dismissing it as "mischief-making only," even though Ivan had expressed alarm. "Did you know" Ciabhan had continued, "that the husband of Faye's serving wench is leaving us? The sooner the better! He is a surly brute, and only here under sufferance. Always he was Leon's man and remains so. The wronged are always dangerous!"

"What of Mati and the child?" asked Ivan.

"The woman is under my protection, but Torr wants the child. That is for them to decide. If it were not for Faye, I would send all three back to Pagons Ton and be done with them!"

It seemed to Ivan that Ciabhan's perception regarding Torr was maybe not so far from the truth. A decision must soon be made. That decision was made for Ivan on his return. Taking leave of each other at the chapel, he and Ciabhan went their separate ways. On his way to his room Ciabhan would habitually stop to talk with the guard who stood sentry over the passageway. However, with the coming celebrations, even guards had been excused all but the most important duties. Commandeered to help with the extra preparations, his station was empty.

As Ivan went down the steps to his own room, he felt a strange unease. As he stepped into the murk, he drew his dagger, but he was just too late to stop the powerful arm that shot across his neck, locking him in a vice-like grip and knocking the knife from his hand. Choking, Ivan battled to free himself. He had heard the knife clatter to the floor, and without it he was at the total mercy of his attacker. Only a few moments more and he would be dead, either from lack of oxygen or a stab to the back! Close to his ear a familiar voice rasped, blasting his senses with alcohol-laden breath. The room spun as Ivan was lifted off his feet, his air almost gone. "Prepare to die, monk, for none can hear!" Images of Faye, Ciabhan and even Mati flashed before his eyes as the voice continued: "The Templar dog is next!"

Frantically Ivan clawed at the arms that threatened to squeeze the life from him, and, in a last desperate move, he forced his lean but flexible body into a violent twist. Raking his nails into the bare arms across his throat, he felt his assailant's skin come away in strips as they crashed to the ground, taking the small table and its contents with them. Ivan, nimble and light, scrabbled for his dagger, having the advantage of speed over the heavier man, who lay winded, grunting like a stuck pig on his back, at Ivan's mercy. Straddling the stricken man with knee thrust firmly into his ribs, Ivan held his knife to his would-be murderer's throat. Triumphant, he smiled into the eyes of the writhing Torr. "Whose turn to die now?" croaked Ivan, smiling. With deliberate and terrible intent he pressed the blade down onto the shaking man's jugular. "Make your peace with God, man. Prepare to pay the ferryman. Your day is done!"

The fear in Torr's eyes found no pity from Ivan, who regarded him contemptuously. Savouring the moment before he rid himself of this fool once and for all, Ivan had not heard Ciabhan's footsteps above him until Ciabhan's sword was thrust into his line of vision, alongside his own dagger. With total lack of sympathy, Ciabhan nicked the terrified Torr's neck with the point of his weapon, loosing the tiniest trickle of blood to run down into his ear. At the same time a patch of wet spread on the floor beneath the terrified Torr's breeches.

Disregarding the wretch at his feet, Ciabhan spoke casually: "He's hardly worth soiling your blade for, my friend. He's an idiot! Is it surprising that his wife chooses to leave him? In fact," said Ciabhan, reaching into his tunic, "take this for your betrayal!" Scornfully he tossed a purse of coins onto Torr's heaving stomach. Turning to Ivan, he said, "Spare the dog, my friend, for I'll not have my wedding day tainted by his treacherous blood! It is fortunate that I lingered awhile in the passageway – a moment longer and I would have heard nothing."

Ivan, still protecting his throbbing throat, wasn't convinced that sparing this idiot was the wisest thing, and the next few minutes confirmed his doubts. How he wished he had slit him from ear to ear!

Struggling onto all fours, Torr sneered through his humiliation, "You think me a fool, Templar? Ask the Raven here just how he spent his time in your absence!"

Ciabhan had stooped to leave under the low arch, but his back tensed and he turned slowly. In one deft movement he seized the quivering Torr and dragged him to his feet. Pushing his face into that of Torr, he said, "And what, pray, do you dare tell me that I know not already? Be very, very sure before you speak. It could be the last sound you ever make!" Torr's brutish features turned into a fearful mask. "Well?" said Ciabhan coldly, tightening his grip.

Pointing at Ivan, Torr spluttered his fury: "There! The foreigner you call friend – he is the betrayer! – he and your betrothed. It was my wife who picked the ring from the floor – such a night of passion that your whore didn't even miss it!" His bloodshot eyes flicked between them as he vented his spleen on the two men, declaring his hatred of Faye and her protectors both. "You have been cuckolded here by the man you call friend, and the wife of Leon, my true master!" Ciabhan released him as if touching poison, and Torr slid down the wall, stammering with fear as he buckled to the floor. "Butcher me, for I care not. You already possess my wife! But ask Faye of Pagons Ton how the emerald came to shatter, for therein lies the truth!"

In laboured bursts the breathing of the three men cut through the silence that had suddenly descended, while from outside came the sound of stone on steel as a guard sharpened his knife. Ivan stared blindly ahead, not really seeing. Ciabhan's back was to him. Motionless, his friend faced the wall where moments before he had pinned Torr. He seemed to have stopped breathing. Over and over in Ivan's head the word 'cuckold' boomed. It bounced from the walls, echoing its mockery at its brooding, silent victim.

A fly landed on Ciabhan's shoulder. Dark against the tan kidskin, it edged boldly beneath his hair. Only when Ciabhan finally moved did it rise, buzzing around his head, where he flicked it irritably from his face. Ivan tried to speak but Ciabhan stopped him. Instead he crouched beside Torr and slid the blade of his knife across the pale man's lips. Speaking in a voice thick with menace, he threatened, "Return then to your master, but methinks I'll have that evil tongue first!" Torr convulsed with fear, but Ciabhan continued hissing into his ear, "Be warned, come within sight of Compton Berry ever again and you will die, along with your son who stays here as a hostage! As for your accusations, think you that I would leave the woman I love with any but the man I trust, while the like of you exist?" Ciabhan spat his disgust at the wretch. "Know also, fool, that the emerald ring of which you speak and which you seem to know so well, was shattered long before it was stolen from me. There is no deceit to be found in its damage."

With disgust he slammed his sword back into its scabbard and made to go as Ivan finally managed to speak: "The coward intended to kill us both, waiting until the guard was absent."

Ciabhan's reply was unexpected in its generosity and left Ivan speechless once more. "My dear Ivan, make no mistake, I miss nothing – nothing at all! What is done is done, and you need not torture yourself over that which cannot be changed! He nodded towards Torr, still moaning amongst the debris. "Now do as you will with the dullard as long as he is out of my sight, for I will have nothing spoil my day!"

Neither Mati nor Faye had any idea of the incident that had taken place earlier. But as Ciabhan passed Mati on his way to Faye's chamber, he informed her curtly, "Your husband has been removed from this household because of his intent to murder. Now mark this well, madam, if he shows his face within sight of these walls again, he will die!" Uninterested in her bafflement, he brusquely asked that he and Faye remain undisturbed, and then he was gone.

Mati, when able again to breathe, immersed herself in his familiar smell. She sighed long with relief: "Oh, sweet release!" At last she was free to enjoy her dreams.

Slightly ajar, the door allowed light to shine through the small gap. Ciabhan could see Faye, her head bowed as if in prayer. He hesitated a moment, loath to disturb her peace, but as he pushed the door open she looked up, a wide smile spreading across her face. "My Lord, what brings you here at this time? Is it not bad luck to see your betrothed the night before the wedding?" She held her hands out in welcome.

He brushed aside her concerns and smiled in return. "That is for the superstitious only." He took her ringless hand. "I have something beautiful for you to wear tomorrow." Into her hand he dropped the ring. Within a plain unadorned gold setting lay the most exquisite emerald. Cleverly cut, the oval shape had been designed so as to resemble the leaves that dripped within the very heart of the green forest. "This befits you more, Faye – a perfect stone to symbolise our own new beginning." He looked towards her dressing table where the shattered emerald glittered, no longer a whole stone, and held together only by the gold setting that encircled it. Ciabhan picked it up. "Come," he said, as strong arms guided her into the keen evening air.

Above them, the heavens sparkled as if sprinkled with diamonds, while below, people scurried like beetles. The flares reminded her of the ghostly green light that emanated from glow-worms in dark hedgerows on September evenings. There was something strange about Ciabhan this evening, as if his mind were on other things. He had looked at her with sad eyes. Now they stood silent together, high above everything. Fleetingly the thought that maybe he knew of her betrayal made her shiver in his arms. Their breath came in little white puffs over the deep violet of the woods.

He opened his hand; in the darkness the fractured stone lay like a shadow in his palm. His next words made her pray that darkness hid her guilty tears: "In moments of despair, Faye, your image in these depths comforted me. I have no desire to see you as a hundred splintered shards! This ring has served its purpose!" Swinging his arm he flung the ring as far as he could out and over the purple treetops, over the same ground that Ivan had retrieved it from when it had slipped from her finger. Then she had panicked; now she was glad it had gone. No longer would it be a constant reminder of guilt. Ciabhan himself had seen fit to bury its memory.

For Ciabhan, discarding the emerald at last exorcised the nightmare. Then he'd seen emeralds falling like the rain. Even then he knew the dream was a forewarning. He had been allowed to see already the betrayal. Strangely he felt as if a burden had been lifted from him, and with that acceptance he no longer cared who had taken the ring or for what purpose. What he did know for certain was that in his absence the ring had brought nothing but angst to those he loved so much. Faye and Ivan would endure no suffering at his hands.

Decked with autumn greenery, the little chapel wore its finery with pride. All the golds of the spectrum blazed, through pale washed-out lemon and orange to rich russet; daisies of Michaelmas blended cheerful colour with dusty green leaves and bronze foliage, and berries of every hue. From the outside gate to the chapel door, boughs and autumnal fruits decorated arches, walls and doorways.

Villagers bearing gifts and good wishes for the couple filled the pathways around Compton Berry with chattering, while merry sounds of music drifted through rustling woods. Household servants ran about their duties, arms laden with victuals for the banquet that would follow, while, in the heated kitchen area, cooks sweated and swore as they toiled.

A simple ceremony had been the wish of both Faye and Ciabhan – a solemnising of their love for each other with a simple blessing of the holy Church on their union. Ciabhan was still very much a Christian man, respecting the rites of the holy Roman Church. Not for nothing had he sought official recognition for Faye's divorce.

With these wishes of his friend in mind, Ivan had planned the marriage rites. Ciabhan and Faye wanted the vows to reflect the unique bond between them, a forbidden love that had transcended and survived, driven by fate alone. They would take the sacrament and the body and blood of Christ and, as Ivan made the sign of the cross, they would pledge each other their troth.

Over the last few days, Ivan's fortitude had taken a battering, leaving him emotionally and spiritually raw. Today's celebrations had to be perfect, for early tomorrow he would leave Compton Berry for ever.

Weakly the morning sun struggled above the window recess, casting its light across the little altar. Ivan's glossy head and olive complexion contrasted starkly with the white cloak he wore today for the first time – a symbol of fresh beginnings. Only the dark smudges beneath his eyes betokened sleepless nights. On the sparkling linen and lace altar cloth he had placed the bloodied pieces of girdle that had once circled Ciabhan's waist. The white linen was pristine as it lay against frayed brown pieces of tapestry, though in places Faye's delicately embroidered symbols were still bright. The mulberry fruits were ruby on what remained; and where the broadsword dripped red blood, if one looked closely, the prayer for the wearer's safety could still be read.

On his knees Ivan rested his forehead on the bloody remnant as he called upon God for guidance and strength. Forgiveness he would have to wait for! Before him this day loomed his last act in the play destiny had planned for him. There had been an innocent beginning and an exciting middle, and here he was at its bitter end. Ivan sighed with resignation and rose to prepare his composure.

Epilogue:

Here the story of Faye, Ciabhan and Ivan concludes, the paths of fate having woven its threads of destiny . . . .

No man can change our path of life.
No woman, priest or fair brave knight
Can destiny confuse.
So think awhile all you who pass,
That love alone is made to last;
Be true to whom you choose.

Alone with just Mati to help her into the beautiful gown, Faye admired her reflection in the mirror. The fabric Ciabhan had bought her had been sewn by Mati into the most lovely of gowns, and a plain wreath of flowers and leaves circled and entwined through her loose hair. Although stunning in her simplicity, Faye suddenly lacked confidence and turned to her maid for reassurance. "Mati, am I really worthy at all of My Lord's devotion?"

Mati answered her patiently: "Faye, Ciabhan is the handsomest knight in all Christendom, and he awaits you. Methinks you had better not delay – even the most perfect of men possess a limit to their patience! Now hurry, before he tires of your tardiness!"

Faye kissed her dear Mati, hugged her close, and, in an aura of sweet vanilla, proceeded down to where her love waited.

Faye stood in front of a poised Ivan with her dauntless knight, and with the respect due to Ciabhan's status, Ivan married them as the congregation cheered and clapped their approval.

It was much later that Ivan could even remember the glorious couple in front of him – Faye's golden gown, the milky pearls at her throat, and Ciabhan's cross swinging low from her neck. Placing the ragged cloth over their entwined hands, he had noticed a new ring, slightly surprised that once again it was an emerald. How the previous sea-green stone had tormented him!

Faye smiled radiantly up at him, and accepted his kiss of friendship. Deep in her eyes there was no regret, but love for the man she had just married. Ivan clasped Ciabhan's hand – the hand he had held through so many trials – and spoke the hardest words he had ever uttered: "Ciabhan, at last you have the happiness you so deserve. I wish you both, my dearest friends, all the happiness in the world."

Ciabhan returned his friend's wishes: "A man could hope for no greater comrade than you, dear Ivan. In triumph and in despair you have been my friend. I pray God will give you as much happiness as I have been blessed with."

With Faye's hand in his, Ciabhan led his wife from the chapel.

Breaking with tradition, Ciabhan had lingered at the banquet only as long as was polite. Catching the normal procession to the bedchamber off guard, he whisked a surprised Faye quickly out of the hall, laughing as revellers scrambled up the stairs after the newly-weds. The custom was for them to be present as their master presented his bride to their marital bed. Ciabhan, however, was having none of it. Sweeping the giggling Faye into his arms, he neatly sidestepped the unwanted visitors and nimbly stepped into the room. In one movement he kicked shut the door while still holding tightly in his arms the highly amused Faye. To the sound of disappointment outside the door, he carried her to the bed, where gently he put her down in a cloud of gold.

With a mock sigh of relief, he looked down at her. "Well, wife, at least we have some privacy. I had no intention of letting an audience in!"

Faye smoothed her crumpled gown and, with an air of deliberation, scolded him: "And did you not think to ask your wife her opinion on this, sir?"

Later as they sat together sharing wine, they savoured the joke, laughing at their foolishness.

Faye presented her gift of their story to him. Although it was still not quite finished, she promised it would continue. "This is for you, my love – our story. Read it when you will."

It was with no haste that they finally climbed beneath the covers. For too long they had waited for this moment, and they were about to enjoy a long and passionate night. At last in each other's arms, there would be no hurry to their love-making.

The great hall of feasting had long fallen into silence before Ciabhan and Faye at last slept. With her head on his chest, watching him sleep, Faye listened to the heartbeat of the man she loved. If she slept herself, she remembered not, for she was sure she had counted each and every one of those beats.

As the first cock crowed, long before the hazy dawn, Ivan was already on his way. Winding up the long drive, he rode as on so many occasions, with no lightness of spirit this time, no enthusiasm for a day's hunt with his friend, but with a heavy heart that dragged and pulled at his soul as he stared straight ahead.

Across his lap, the sword rested in its scabbard of strong black leather studded with silver and reinforced with iron bands for durability. Also the inside was iron-lined for added strength. The weapon itself was of fine Spanish workmanship, its grip bound in thick burgundy leather strips. Along the guard was engraved the name of Ivan's father. The day Ivan had left Rome and his parents' home, his elderly father had presented it proudly to his son, extracting a promise that he use it honourably in the name of Christianity. Looking back at Compton Berry, Ivan ran his fingers along the familiar pattern.

Autumn winds would soon scythe away the last of the tenuous leaves, and the castle, snug in its valley, would once more be visible, for now it lay still out of sight from the high road. Light from the rising sun reflected off the silver studding on the sword and danced under Ivan's chin and on the gold chain just visible above his woollen tunic. Against the black clothing his skin glowed with summer's well-being, an outward picture of health. None who saw the Raven that morning would guess that inside he was dying.

For a moment he faltered at the thought of leaving behind all he had come to love in that peaceful valley. Carrying the scent of the sea on its breath, the wind reached the nostrils of his restless horse, who tossed his mane, ready to be gone. The wind had loosed strands of black hair from its fastening at the back of Ivan's neck and whipped it across his cheeks, stinging him back to the present.

At his side the excited voices of his travelling companions sought directions from him. "To the sea, master?" they asked.

Ivan smiled, not out of pleasure but irony. What an exotic trio they must look to passers-by as they emerged from the Devon mists – a dark man all in black and two gaudy Turkish men-at-arms. He had not wanted company, but Ciabhan had insisted on them, for his friend's protection, and Ivan would not offend.

He crossed himself and mouthed a last silent goodbye;

his prayers had all been said. Reaching into his cape he caressed the lapis brooch pinned to the inside of his cloak – Faye's last gift. Then, turning the horse's head to the sea, Ivan faced the misty horizon. "Aye, my friends, to the sea!"

Ivan had many hours to reflect on his leaving Compton Berry. The controlled sadness of his friend cut him to the bone deeper than any sword thrust; the pain scalded and tore at his being. He dared not look back in the direction from whence he had come for fear of seeing Ciabhan's face, for he would have turned and sped back to all he loved.

The loneliness and pain seemed a little further from his mind as Ivan pulled the sparse covers to his neck after making the shores of France. Attempting to rest before the next leg of his long journey, his travelling companions had long been asleep. Gladder of their company than he had thought, they lightened his gloom at times with cheery laughter.

The day was still bright and cold, and night not yet upon them, when, without warning, the longest most mournful wail rent the quiet outside the small country inn. Inhuman and not of this world, it filled the void of his head. Looking around all was calm; nothing else stirred or seemed disturbed by the awful sound. Disquieted, he took time to still the turmoil in his soul. Slowly he drifted back to an uneasy sleep, thankfully unaware of the terrible tragedy unfolding around the serene heart of Ciabhan of Compton Berry.

The dull thump of the arrow meant for him was all Ciabhan heard as it thudded into Faye's chest, killing her instantly. She had fallen to the ground from her little mare without a sound. Death felled his lovely Faye in beautiful slow motion; it had taken her with a terrible elegance. At times he couldn't hold back the floodgates of that dreadful day, and memories like demons, baiting and tormenting his soul, devoured his very being. His keen senses had sparked at the drawing of the assassin's bow as it released its deadly arrow, but in the half-second it took to turn to Faye she was already dead.

Ciabhan welcomed the continuous pain, for he blamed himself alone. His vow to protect the woman he loved had failed miserably; in his care she had perished, days after becoming his wife.

Trance-like were the days following the tragedy. A shroud of misery descended on Compton Berry, and an unseen hand day by day tightened its hold and squeezed the very essence from the stones of the deathly castle. Ciabhan existed only, a figure detached from reality, as his heart had been detached from its core when the killer's arrow tore it from his chest.

Without Ivan, Alain's support was essential and the young knight became his pillar of strength. "Sir?" He asked the question still with disbelief. "Where would you lay your lady to rest?"

Crossing to the window, Ciabhan's gaze followed the curve of the lane below. Bearing right, a spur led into an overhung dark gap at the wood's edge. Ciabhan heard Alain fidget behind him, but his mind was already in the glade where Faye danced before his eyes, a vision in the rain. At last he spoke: "There is but one place where she shall rest – a place of peace and beauty for my wife."

The words had come matter-of-factly, but Ciabhan's appearance belied the practical reply. Shockingly, his handsome face was haggard and drawn. The mouth so ready to smile in Faye's presence had set once more in its hard line, and the previously luminous eyes were dull and expressionless. Cruel sorrow had turned this once fine-looking knight into a shell of his former self. Alain barely recognised the greying pallor of the man who turned to face him.

Swifts still returned to Compton Berry in the springtime. Screeching in the still blue of evening, they swooped and dipped and raised their young, leaving all too quickly as autumn approached. The blackbird still harmonised with her mate, its song the first of the new day and the last at night, the joyful lyrics filling forest and hearts. Skylarks still rose from the buttercup-filled fields where Faye had walked so often. Jubilant, they rose high into summer skies, small chests bursting with song. Far from view, their song would carry for miles.

Alone, Ciabhan still took Faye's beloved Bella Donna to the high meadows, smiling a rare secret smile when the bird returned to settle and preen once more on his wrist. Mati still fed the tame raven that daily visited the castle walls. Unable to strut, the damaged but once magnificent bird huddled on the heights until the day he came no more. In the glade the owl protected her chick beneath the rafters of the deserted lodge. Sweeping low through the doorless opening with beak full of food, her huge all-seeing eyes spotted the great black bird flailing on the ground as it gasped for air. The once noble raven, unable to lift its head any longer, drew its last breath and expired on the soft green mound beneath its broken body as the forest fell quiet.

Rain pattered through the trees in sparkling droplets and gradually darkened with moss the square of limestone that bore the words:

Our story, far from being done,
Will live each day, my love, my sun;
And when death calls for us to part,
You'll live for ever in my heart.